Dancing Through the Past

Adrian Fosbery

Contents

Prologue

Relationships are built by the bond between two persons. It is earned by trust and deepened by love. However, once broken, it would be difficult to establish again.

Theirs was like any other play. A heart-fluttering kind of make-believe. And how she wished that what they had was real. She had been friends with him for a short period, but it was enough to fall for his charms.

Everything was perfect about Dereck. His height, looks, and character. The only problem was that his eyes were in a different direction. He was only interested in her best friend, Angelica. That's why he always tagged along wherever they went. How foolish she was to think she could stay by his side by being "just friends" when it was the last thing she had ever imagined.

"Hey, Jamaica, I'm planning to watch a movie. Do you want to come with me?" he asked casually as they strolled down the side of the streets. "Angelica said she needs to meet her tutor and review for the exam so it's only the two of us."

"Really?" Her eyes glistened like a little girl's, and she smiled widely. It will only be the two of us!

Dereck smiled back, then stopped at a donut shop to buy some. It was their daily routine whenever they went home together. They ate the donuts, took a train, and separated when he reached his stop.

She settled herself on a vacant seat, and he sat beside her. Jamaica closed her eyes, hoping to sleep since her stop was fifteen stops away from where they rode. However, her senses heightened. She could hear his breathing and even the beating of his heart. She could also sense that he was moving closer to offer his shoulder for her to lean on.

It was a battle. Her heart and mind were in chaos. Should she stay in her position or lean on his shoulder? What should she do?

Jamaica felt he stood and heard his footsteps when the doors opened. And he was gone. She immediately opened her eyes and breathed out the air she didn't realize she was holding in.

And it was like that every single day.

She didn't want to give in. Why? It was simple. Because there was no label, and his action proved it.

Jamaica was already checking herself in front of a full-length mirror. "Okay, you're already good." She smiled and then walked out of her bedroom. "Mom! Dad! I'm going now." Jamaica was running down the stairs.

"Are you with Angelica?" asked her dad while watching television. He did not even bother to give her a single glance.

"I-uh, yeah! She's with me. We'll watch a movie and have dinner together."

"Go home early, okay?" her mother, Claudine, uttered.

"Yup. Bye now!" She ran to the door and made a left turn to the next street, where the jeepneys passed. Jamaica patiently waited for a jeepney with fewer passengers so she could sit at the end of the vehicle. She couldn't contain her happiness that it would be just the two of them.

Jamaica arrived at the park. She took her time watching her surroundings as she sat on a bench and waited for Dereck. The calm wind made her eyes heavy. Yawning, she closed them for a while, not realizing she had already fallen asleep.

"Jamaica?" he called, tapping her shoulder. "Jamaica, wake up," Dereck said, trying not to laugh.

Slowly, she opened her eyes and saw his handsome, smiling face. "Why are you sleeping here? Come on, let's go somewhere else."

They stepped inside a building and walked straight to a classroom where a wall was covered with full-length mirrors. "Is this a dance studio?" Jamaica looked around and saw that only a few chairs were at the four corners of the room. "What are we doing here?"

"What do you think?" Dereck flashed his signature grin which made her nervous. Oh, no.

"Oh, yes." He laughed, enjoying her reaction. "I'll teach you how to dance the waltz."

Jamaica tried to run away but because she has short legs Dereck caught up with her with only two wide steps and grabbed her by the collar. "I don't want to dance!"

"Come on, I'll bring you to my father's wedding party, that's why I need to teach you." He said in a slightly annoyed voice. Letting her go, he added. "Or I can bring Angelica. I just need to ask her. She already knows how to dance so I don't need to teach her."

He knows where it hurts and hits her on purpose. She hid the frown on her face as she bent her head down.

"You're pouting now?" Dereck held his hand out. "Let's practice. The party is on Saturday already."

"Already?" He nodded and then played the song using the remote control. They danced to the music with Jamaica constantly stepping on his foot until she finally got it right, she thought.

Saturday came and Jamaica told her parents that, again, she would be with Angelica and have a sleepover at her place. Joselito and Claudine didn't have any problem with that as long as Jamaica updates them on where she is.

She was in her and Dereck's meeting place. She instantly saw him when she arrived. Dereck was standing tall in his black suit with a white undershirt. His slick back hair was neat and made him even more dashing. Jamaica got insecure, she couldn't bring herself to walk toward him.

He saw her and approached her where she was standing. "Why are you here? Did you arrive just now?" Dereck checked his wristwatch and then glanced at her. "What are you wearing?" She looked at herself. Dressed in a casual black blouse and skirt with black casual shoes, which was her usual attire. "Are you going to a funeral? Tsk." He grabbed her hand.

They were already in a boutique renting a gown for her and having her make-up for a party the next thing she knew. Jamaica dressed in a white above-knee dress paired with white wedge shoes. "That's better," Dereck said while he took her picture on his phone. "Let's go."

The two of them arrived at a famous hotel and entered the ballroom, surprising everyone, especially his father, Mr. Sy. "Son! You came!" He walked towards them at the entrance.

Dereck let out an exasperated sigh, "Hi, dad."

"Who is this lovely lady you brought?" Mr. Sy smiled at her.

She smiled back, bowing her head a little. "Good evening, sir." Jamaica greeted, but Dereck held her wrist to stop her.

"You don't need to know who she is. I just brought her here since you kept asking me to come. We'll go home after eating." He dragged her to the buffet table.

What? Why did he teach me how to dance when we won't even do it? Jamaica thought while looking at the dance floor filled with the other guests.

The two sat on vacant seats and started eating everything on their plates. Dereck chuckled as he watched Jamaica finish her food with gusto. "Wait here. I'll get us something to drink." He stood up and made his way back to the table.

He came back holding a glass of wine and orange juice in his hands a minute later. "Here you go."

Jamaica gladly received it and drank every ounce of the juice. "I'm done. Can we go home now?"

"I'll just finish this drink," He said when it was already his fifth glass.

Dereck got drunk, and it left her no choice but to ask for help in putting him in a room. "Hah! Why are you so heavy?!" She breathed heavily after carrying him to the bed.

Standing at the end of the bed, she threw him on the soft mattress. "I'll go home now, okay?" Jamaica looked at her wristwatch. It was already her curfew. "See you on Monday."

She was about to walk away when Dereck grabbed her left hand and pulled her beside him. "H-hey, D, what are you doing?" He turned, embracing her. "Angelica..." She tried to push him off, but his hold wouldn't falter. Instead, it kept on tightening like a cuff.

"I'm not Angelica, okay? Can you please let me go? I need to go home."

"No..." he mumbled, "don't leave me." He weakly lifted his head and opened his eyes. He said nothing else. And that made Jamaica scared. Scared she might give in. She shut her eyes tightly, distracting herself from thinking other thoughts.

"Can I kiss you?"

Her eyes widened, surprised. But before she could even answer, his soft, heated lips made their way to capture hers.

Chapter 1

Seven years later.

"Mommy, Mommy, wake up... I'm hungry." The little hand of her six-year daughter kept poking her face.

"Five more minutes, baby, let mommy sleep more." The mattress was so fluffy that she sank in, fighting her way to separate from it. Turning her head to the side, a ray of sunlight passing through the window gently hit her face.

"Mommy..."

"Are Papsi and Mamita not downstairs?"

"Nope. They went outside to exercise." Her daughter lies down on her back.

Jamaica uttered a simple prayer. Thank You for this day. Help us in everything we'll do with the strength You lent us. Amen. Then slowly, she opened her brown eyes, meeting the pitch-black ones of Camila, who was smiling from ear to ear. "Good morning, Mommy!" She began jumping up and down on the bed.

"Good morning, baby!" Jamaica sat up and kissed her little girl on the top of her head. "Let's go down now." She swiftly moved her legs out of bed and stood up, carrying her daughter downstairs.

They headed straight to the kitchen and placed Camila on a high chair. "What do you want for breakfast, sweetheart?"

"Bacon and eggs!" She giggled excitedly.

"Okay, princess, wait for Mommy." Jamaica tied her hair up and started cooking. She grabbed a pan, took out the bacon and eggs inside the refrigerator, and fried them.

The two of them had been staying in Canada with her parents. They migrated when she discovered she was pregnant with Camila. After her pregnancy, Jamaica continued her studies. She finished her fourth year in medical school and then continued her general surgery residency at Toronto General Hospital.

She finished cooking the bacon and eggs and plated them. She placed the plate on the kitchen counter along with the rice bowl. Scooping rice to Camila's plate, her phone rang. Jamaica checked the screen and answered. "Hi, Stephen? You called?"

"Hi, Claire. I was thinking..." he paused, "Do you want to work here in our hospital? You know you can continue residency here. If you want to?"

"Why do you need help?"

"Well...actually yes, we need doctors in the pediatric department. If you'll say yes, I will recommend you."

"I'll get back to you, Stephen. I'll ask permission first from Mom and Dad."

"I already asked them." He said with a chuckle.

Jamaica heartily laughed. "Looks like you planned it well, huh?"

"Of course. It has been my goal to recruit you to our hospital. So, when do you plan to leave? I'll pick you up at the airport."

"Wait, I haven't agreed yet."

"Aww, anyway, just let me know and I'll pick you up at the airport."

"Okay, bye."

"Bye. Tell Camila I said hi."

Jamaica placed her phone down on the counter after the call. "Mommy, is that Daddy Stephen?"

"Baby," She sighed. "Can you not call Uncle Stephen, daddy?

"But-"

"Do you want to see him again?"

"Yes!"

They heard the sound of the door opening and closing. "Papsi! Mamita!" Camila called her grandparents as she rushed toward them with a hug.

"Good morning, cupcake. Did you have breakfast? We bought some cakes on our way back." Joselito and Claudine were dressed in loose red couple shirts and gray sweatpants matched with running shoes.

"Yehey, cakes!" Camila opened the box and looked for her favorite flavor, strawberry cheesecake. She took it out herself and carried it to the kitchen to eat with her bacon and eggs.

Jamaica grabbed the box of cakes, chuckling to herself. She walked back to the kitchen and put it on the kitchen counter. "Mom, Dad, Stephen asked if I wanted to go back to the Philippines and continue my residency there."

"Yes, he mentioned that to us and we're good with that," Joselito told her daughter.

She bit her lower lip. "I want to go home but I'm afraid. What if I meet him again," Jamaica glanced at Camila. "I don't know what will I tell him if that happens."

"Sweetheart," Claudine approached her and held her on both shoulders. "You should tell him the truth."

"What if he gets angry?"

"You should be prepared for that. The moment you decided you wanted to live here, you should have thought of that."

"The only thing I'll advise you to do is to pray, sweetheart. All your problems that even us couldn't help you with. Knees and floor. Remember that."

Jamaica gave a small smile. She truly appreciated having such wonderful parents. They never left her even though she gave them too many disappointments.

She followed what her father advised her and after a fervent prayer, she had made up her mind.

Arriving in Manila around lunchtime, they saw Stephen waiting for them, holding a placard in his hand. "Claire! Camila!" He called, standing about six feet tall. He ran and met them halfway, then grabbed their suitcases.

"Daddy Stephen!" Camila raised her little arms, asking to be carried. Jamaica glared at her daughter's action. "Baby, I told you not to call Uncle Stephen like that." She faced him and said, "She missed you a lot." She took the bags from him as they continued walking towards the exit. They reached Stephen's car, and Stephen loaded their luggage in the compartment while Jamaica and Camila sat in the passenger's seat.

Stephen hopped into the driver's seat and started the engine. "Do you want to eat first, or do you want to go straight home?"

"Drop us home. We can order later." She looked down at Camila, who was already sleeping on her chest.

"Okay. I'll just go out again to buy groceries and cook for you. No buts." He said before she could complain. "You can start to work on Monday. Everyone in the General Surgery Department is already excited to meet you."

"Really?" She smiled weakly as she turned her head to the window and watched the view outside. Jamaica was not at all excited. Instead, she felt scared that she-they might come across Dereck. She doesn't know what to do. Whooo. I'll just let God be in control.

A week later, Jamaica decided to visit the hospital where she'll work. She left Camila to her former nanny, Yaya Mel. She took the bus and got off at the bus stop near the hospital. Taking a walk to the building, she noticed an old man who looked unwell so she approached him. "Hello, Sir. Are you alright?"

The old man looked surprised to see her. "I-I'm fine, dear."

"Are you also going to the hospital?" He nodded his head. The two of them entered the hospital's lobby and she assisted him to the emergency room.

Doctors, nurses, patients, and all kinds of people from different walks of life were inside the hospital. It was overwhelming to her every time she met someone and helped them. Jamaica went to the information desk to ask for assistance. "Hi, I'm Jamaica and I'm the new resident in the General Surgery Department."

"Ah, yes," the desk staff handed her I.D. "Doctor Stephen Sy instructed us to tell you to meet him first. He's in the Pediatric Department on the third floor."

"Thank you." She got inside the elevator and hit the button to the third floor. Jamaica saw the nurses' station and asked for Stephen's office.

Standing in front of his office, she read. Doctor Stephen Brown, Pediatric Surgeon. She knocked on the door and opened it then peeked inside. "Stephen?"

"Hey, Claire. You're finally here!" Stephen stood up from his table and opened the door widely for her. "Come inside. Do you want to drink coffee or tea?"

Jamaica shook her head. "I'm good. I just wanted to see you and at the same time visit before I start next week."

"Oh, yeah. I'll introduce you to the other doctors and nurses." Stephen put his hands on her shoulders and gently pushed her outside.

They were at the nurses' station and he introduced the nurses one by one. He pointed to the nurse who had a slim figure. "That one is Nurse Angelica Garcia. I call her Angge, sometimes."

Angelica turned around and their eyes immediately met. "Jamaica?!"

"Angelica? Is that you?" I thought he was mentioning a different person.

The nurse stepped out off the counter and grabbed her hands. "What happened? What are you doing here? Why did you stop your communication with us?"

She felt awkward and unsure if she should answer her questions. "I'll tell you some other time."

"Have you seen Dereck? Have you met him already?" Angelica innocently asked.

Jamaica swallowed the invisible lump in her throat. Hearing his name made her so uncomfortable. This is what I was talking about.

Dereck just finished directing his play on Broadway. He decided to go home straight to Manila after the play's three-month run. He had been in the Philippines for a week already and helped in managing the dance school that he and his friend, Adrian, established before he flew to New York a year ago.

As he looked outside the window and watched the people walking by, he thought of Jamaica.

For the last seven years, she never left his mind. And his heart. I should forget you already. My heart is tired of waiting when will you be coming back. He turned his head to the script on top of his desk. It was a story he wrote for her.

"Oooohhh... What script is this, Direk?" A young lady picked it up and scanned the pages.

"Rosette, give me that!" He grabbed the paper from her and immediately hid it inside the drawer.

"It's a good story. Why don't you produce it into a play?"

"No. I just wrote it but I don't have a plan on doing it as a play."

"Why?" His eighteen-year-old actress asked. "I wish I could play the female lead. It would be my first project as the main lead." She clasped her hands together and looked at him hoping he would change his mind.

Dereck ignored her. Instead, he gave her an instruction. "Help me find someone who can help us in promoting this dance school. We need at least twenty students to enroll when we open the classes."

"I know someone. She's my co-worker at MC Events." Rosette took out her phone from the pocket of her jeans and messaged her friend. An hour later, a lady around Rosette's age, arrived at the school.

"Hey, Rics!" Rosette ran to her and hugged her tightly. Because Rica was small and a little bit chubby, Dereck remembered Jamaica. His heart ached but he chose to deny his feeling and ignore it.

"Why did you call me? What do you need?"

"Can you help us do a campaign for our school's event? We need at least twenty enrollees when we open the classes."

"Give me the details and I'll help you create a marketing strategy."

"How much is your fee, Rics?" Rosette asked all of a sudden. Dereck elbowed her lightly. She glanced at him and saw him mouthing, Ask that later.

"It's okay. Just a meal will do."

They walked inside the office and Rica started creating the materials for the campaign.

Another hour passed by and Rica was able to create a photo and video advertisement. "It's finished. You can post this to your page to promote the upcoming event. As for the other days, just edit the date on the project file."

"Thanks." Dereck shyly said. "Let's go. I'll treat you two to lunch."

The three of them stepped out of the dance school and searched for a nearby eatery. "Rics, are you sure you don't want to eat in a fancy restaurant?"

"I'm good. Anywhere is fine." She gave a small smile as they walked under the sun.

"Let's go here!" Rosette pointed at the eatery she has just seen. "Maybe the food here is nice."

"No, let's go to the other restaurant. I'm a regular there." Dereck told them and walked first, leaving them behind.

Rosette ran to catch up to him holding Rica on the wrist. "H-hey!"

It was a small restaurant but the ambiance was nice. Dereck preferred eating there because the foods were delicious and the customer service was top-notch. "What do you want to order?" He called a waiter and one came running.

Rica was reading the menu and then gave her orders. "I would like one Pork Sinigang, one Sisig, one Palabok, five Pork Barbecue, one Beef Caldereta, one Grilled Liempo, and five rice."

Rosette and Dereck were surprised by her order. "That's only for me, okay?"

"I would like one Kare-Kare and one rice," said Rosette.

Clearing his throat, Dereck ordered Adobo and rice for himself.

"What are your drinks? Ma'am, Sir?"

"Is water, okay?" He asked and the two nodded. "That all."

The waiter left to hand their orders to the kitchen and then came back with a holding tray. It has a pitcher of water and three glasses.

While waiting for their food, Dereck drank water from his glass. Suddenly, he received a text message from Angelica.

Hey, I met Jamaica.

He nearly choked and abruptly stood as he read that one sentence. Shit!

Chapter 2

Another day in the hospital and Jamaica arrived in time before the morning rounds. She passed by the nurses' station and greeted everyone before going inside the on-call room to put down her things and get ready.

She still had fifteen minutes before eight so she decided to have a quick coffee from the vending machine. There she met Angelica who was choosing what to have. Jamaica stood beside her. "Hey, Jamaica!"

"Good morning."

"Good morning, what would you like to drink?"

"Hot coffee."

Angelica chose the hot coffee for her. "By the way, do you know that Dereck established a dance school? He's even a musical play director and scriptwriter."

Jamaica nodded even though she wanted to roll her eyes. I don't care! She thought. She inhaled deeply then exhaled in a long sigh. I didn't come back here to hear anything about him. She was about to say something when Angelica beat her to it.

"Look!" She flashed her phone at her. "They are opening a new series of classes. Can you join me and enroll in the ballroom class?"

Hearing that, Jamaica burned her tongue in the hot drink she was drinking.

Angelica exclaimed. "Are you alright?"

She nodded as she bit the end of her tongue.

The nurse gave her a drink, the juice she selected from the machine. "Here, drink this."

Jamaica took the bottle and drank the remaining contents of it. "Thanks."

"You're welcome." Angelica took the bottle from her hand and threw it in the bin near the vending machine. "So, what do you think? Do you want to enroll in the class with me?"

She shook her head. "I don't think I can with my schedule right now."

"Oh, okay."

"I have to go now." Jamaica left Angelica standing alone in the corridor. Whew! I got to escape now. But knowing Angelica, she will ask me again until I say yes. She opened her mouth and fanned her tongue as she ran back to their room.

Lunchtime came and Angelica joined Jamaica and Stephen in the cafeteria. "Hello, Doc Stephen, Jamaica." She sat beside her friend and started eating.

"Hey, Nurse Angge. I still can't believe you two were college friends."

"Really?" Angelica smiled. "We were classmates in a subject but we have another friend."

"Where is she right now?"

"Well, he was recently on Broadway but now he's here in the Philippines taking a break. He's managing the dance school he established."

If she could only close her ears, Jamaica already did, just to ignore what her friend was talking about. She doesn't need to know what Dereck had been doing for the past years. She knew to herself she was not fine yet. Her heart hasn't settled yet and she's not denying that.

Angelica turned to her and asked the same question, "Do you want to join me in enrolling in the ballroom dance class?"

"Angel, I already said no."

"But-" her friend pouted. "Can you just help me meet my boyfriend? Can you go with me to the school?"

Jamaica just opened her mouth.

"Please..." Angelica grabbed her right hand and held it tightly.

I might meet him there. She thought. What will I do? Should I just pretend as if nothing happened? Should I tell him everything about Camila?

Biting her lower lip, she sighed. "Fine. I'll go with you."

"Yey!" Angelica embraced her quickly and then continued eating.

Maybe it's time.

"Can I join you, girls?" Stephen asked.

"Nope. It's a girl thing, Doc. Maybe next time."

He heartily chuckled. "If you say so." And took a bite of his food.

Saturday came and it was the night of the dance class. A three-story building stood in front of Jamaica. Wearing a long maxi dress and running shoes, she stared at the establishment, contemplating if she should go inside. It looked abandoned because of the cracks on the wall and some graffiti written on it. Is this the right place?

She took out her phone from the sling bag she had on her body and dialed Angelica's number. She was waiting for an answer until she heard someone call her. "Jamaica!" Speaking of the devil.

Angelica rushed towards wearing her usual clothes, a light purple above the knee dress partnered with white wedges. She was waving as she hurried to hug her. "You came!" She released her then Hooked her arm on Jamaica, she pulled her inside. "Let's go inside."

Nervous of what might happen, Jamaica took courage with her.

There they spotted a slim yet muscular guy dressed in a fitted shirt and jeans. He was behind the information desk reading a book wearing a pair of eyeglasses. He noticed them standing by the door and greeted them, "Good evening, did you enroll in the class?"

"We haven't enrolled yet. Can we still register now?" Angelica asked.

"Sure." The guy passed on a paper to Angelica and Jamaica.

"No. I'm just accompanying her." She nervously laughed the took a glimpse at his name tag. Dave...

Dave gave them a suspicious look then said, "Go upstairs and you'll see the first classroom there. You can open the lights and the fans. The other students are already there. You can just wait for the instructor."

Following the instruction of the guy at the information desk, they went upstairs and looked for the comfort room. "Come on, I'll get changed."

Jamaica followed Angelica to change clothes. Minutes later, she was wearing a black flared dress with black flared heel ballroom dance shoes. "What do you think?" She turned around and then stood in front of the mirror.

"It's nice. It suits you."

Angelica's eyes gleamed when she looked at her friend. "I also brought yours."

"What?" Jamaica exclaimed as she watched her take out another dress from the paper bag.

"Wear this."

"You asked me to just come with you. I don't want to take the class."

Please...please...please..." Angelica tried to act cute. "Just this one time."

"I guess I have no choice." Jamaica's shoulders fell. "How bad can it be?"

Jamaica struggled in wearing the red flared dress and ballroom shoes that Angelica bought for her. "Do I really have to do this?" Dancing was the last thing she wanted to do.

"You look fabulous. Red suits your white skin." Her lips curved into an accomplished grin while her hands were on her hips. "It's the first time I saw you dressed like that."

Though she felt awkward wearing it, she felt happy. The dress fitted her well no one could say she was once pregnant with her daughter.

"Come on. I think the class is already starting." Angelica grabbed her arm and they both stepped out of the comfort room.

They saw the first room and from the open windows by the corridor, Jamaica glanced at the other students. She suddenly heard his voice which made her stop in her tracks. Dereck!

"Why?" Angelica looked back at her. "What's the matter?" She noticed her friend paled. "Are you alright, Jamaica?"

Dereck arrived at the dance school. Dave greeted him and handed the paper with the list of students. "Hey, here are the names of the students."

"Okay, thanks." He took it and headed upstairs. When he entered the classroom, the number of students was un-expected. I guess the advertising campaign worked. "Good evening."

"Good evening." The students replied.

"I guess we can start our first session for this dance class now." He said looking at his wristwatch.

Suddenly, they all heard a knock on the door. "Good evening, sorry we're late."

It was Angelica. Dereck frowned when he saw her. But what surprised him was the one with her. Jamaica! What is she doing here? It was as if he forgot breathing.

Seeing her in the red flared dress made her alluring. She was far from the Jamaica she knew before. Wow! He gulped. Dereck tried to act normal. That everything was normal.

Angelica entered the room with Jamaica and stood in front. He cleared his throat. "Where were we?"

Dereck looked away, trying to ignore her presence and pretend she was not there. "For tonight, we'll study the basic steps of ballroom dancing. Who amongst here doesn't have any idea about ballroom dancing? As in zero-knowledge?"

Other students raised their hands, even Angelica. He glanced at Jamaica and their eyes met. She was the first one to break their eye contact.

"I will show you the basic steps of the ballroom." He turned around and faced the mirrors on the walls. After doing the set of steps, he called someone. "Can anyone show me if you got the steps right?"

No one wanted to volunteer so picked someone. "You, miss, would you care to show us?"

He couldn't deny how overwhelmed he was to see Jamaica again. However, Dereck didn't want her to know that. He smirked seeing how Jamaica's face paled. She glanced at everyone and turned to him. Her eyes were pleading, asking if he could call someone else. Dereck raised an eyebrow and smirked then he slowly shook his head.

Dereck called her out. Me? Her jaw dropped. Oh no! Angelica nudged her and whispered. "Come on, Jamaica, show us your dancing skills."

She shook her head but Angelica kept pushing her to the center. The nervousness she was feeling began building up. She began trembling.

She felt a warm hand grab her cold ones. Jamaica turned and saw Dereck beside her. He placed her left hand on his shoulder blade and then held her right hand. "First, for the men, the leader should place your right hand on the woman, the follower's left shoulder blade at the back of her armpit."

He placed his right arm behind Jamaica's armpit as he described how it was done. "Then, the woman's left hand should be placed at the man's upper arm near the shoulder blade." He slowly and sensually brushed his fingers from her arm to her hand before placing it on his shoulder sending electricity through her whole body.

"The available hand of the leader will then wrap the follower's hand around his. "Like this," explained Dereck. Though others could not see it, Jamaica felt it. He squeezed her hand sending another surge of sparks within her. She turned to her side to hide a blush that was forming on her cheeks.

Jamaica doesn't want to admit it but Dereck's touch still has the same effect on her. "If you're ready. You can dance now." Her heartbeat was getting louder and louder and she could barely notice that the music had already started. She gasped and stopped breathing when Dereck moved closer to her.

Like how he grabbed her hand, it was also sudden when he let her go. As if placing her on a pedestal and then releasing her. She knew she shouldn't be hurt. But it does!

"Those are the basic steps in ballroom dancing. You may choose your partners and practice." Dereck glanced at her with his cold stare like she was a stranger he never wanted to meet.

Jamaica clenched her jaw and maintained a poker face. She heard her phone ring from her sling bag so she took it out. Stepping out of the room, she answered the call. "Hello?

"Hello, Mommy? When are you coming home?" Camila asked over the phone. "Can you buy me chocolates?"

"Did you already finish your chocolates? I just bought that the other day." She baby talked.

Camila giggled loudly. "I love you, Mommy."

"You really know what to say when you want something, huh?"

"I miss you."

Jamaica laughed. "I miss you too. Wait for me at home, okay?"

"Okay. Bye, Mommy!" She sent her a kiss before ending the call.

When she was about to go back inside the room, Jamaica was startled to see Dereck standing by the door with his arms crossed. Her eyes grew in fear. Did he hear us?

She avoided his eyes and walked back inside the room to get her change of clothes.

He didn't want her out of his sight so he kept following her through his gaze. Dereck turned around and saw she was grabbing her things already. She was looking around for Angelica then hurriedly ran to the comfort room then went out in a casual blouse and square pants. Why is she in a rush?

He wanted to follow her but the class was still ongoing. Dereck, stop! What are you doing?! He shook his head and went back inside the room. You're better than this!

Chapter 3

Angelica exited the classroom quietly hoping to see her boyfriend in the office. And she was not wrong. She saw her stepping inside and was about to close the door when she held the doorknob.

Adrian looked behind. He was surprised to see her. "What are you doing here?" He coldly stared at her.

"Why are you avoiding me?" Angelica followed him inside and closed the door.

His attitude scared her. It was her first time seeing him act as if she was not there. As if she was a stranger. He was not saying anything.

"Adrian," she called in a warning tone.

He glanced in her direction and looked straight into her eyes. "Well, I don't want to see you anymore. So I hope this will be the last time you'll come here." Adrian sat on the swivel chair behind a desk and opened the laptop.

Fazed, she marched out of the room and ran upstairs. However, Jamaica was already gone. "Where did she go?"

Angelica tried calling her but it was only ringing. The other students were already leaving so she asked Dereck. "Have you seen Jamaica?"

"She left earlier."

"Why didn't she tell me?"

"She was looking for you but you weren't around."

Angelica remembered that the two used to be close so she asked him. "So, did you two catch up? I bet you also didn't have any news about her."

Dereck cleared his throat. "No. We didn't talk."

"Awww. I thought she would talk to you. She's quiet even at the hospital. But she's always with Doctor Stephen."

His hearing became sensitive. Stephen? Who's that?

Answering his thought Angelica told him. "It's one of the professors in the hospital where we are working. He's the son of the Chairman."

"Are you going home now?" He changed the topic. I couldn't hear anything more about her.

"Yeah. I'll just get changed. You'll drive me home, right?"

He nodded his head.

After dropping off Angelica, Dereck went home. His room-mate, Adrian, was already inside the apartment when he came in. "I just sent Angelica home."

"I didn't ask."

"Just letting you know."

Adrian glared at him and he only smirked. Even though Angelica used to be his first love. Dereck respected that she loved his friend and their relationship was not like theirs. He also knew the reason why Adrian kept on ignoring her. Sadly, he couldn't do anything for them.

He plopped down on the couch and closed his eyes. Image of Jamaica was what he kept seeing. It still surprised him to see her again. After all these years. He shook his head to erase that.

"Are you alright?" His friend placed a cold cup of water on the coffee table.

He sat properly and drank it. "Yeah. I just met someone I know."

Observing him, Adrian didn't ask anymore. "What about the class?"

"It was fine." He remembered Jamaica again. She was so gorgeous in the red flared dress she was wearing. She was more beautiful than before.

For the nth time, random thoughts and questions crossed his mind. Why did she leave? Where did she go? What happened? He couldn't fathom everything.

Seven years ago.

Dereck woke up in an unfamiliar room. Alone. Unclothed and only covered by the blanket, he remembered memories of last night. How he and Jamaica shared one of the most unforgettable moments of his life.

He sat up. "Jamaica?" There was no answer. "Jamaica?" He panicked when he realized she was not there. She left.

Dereck dressed in a hurry. He checked the time on his wristwatch and saw he was already late for school. He reached the apartment and headed towards his bedroom when Adrian asked him. "Hey, where did you go yesterday? Why didn't you go home last night?"

He never said anything and just passed by him.

Opening his closet, Dereck hastily searched for a new shirt and pants then changed the suit he was wearing. He grabbed his bag before running to the bathroom to brush his teeth and wet his hair.

Adrian stopped eating and watched him circle the apartment.

"Bye," Dereck said, then stepped out of the room leaving his friend speechless.

Running late, he reached the university just in time before his second class starts. When he was already inside the classroom, Dereck took out his phone from his pocket and hid it under the table to text Jamaica.

Hey Jamaica, why didn't you wake me up and left me alone?

He expected to receive an immediate answer still there was no text. Jamaica was quick to give replies to his messages. He waited and waited. Huh? Why isn't she texting back? It started to piss him but he ignored it. I don't care if she replies or not.

After the class, he went to see Angelica and ask if Jamaica was with her. "Jamaica didn't come to school today. She said she was not feeling well."

He got worried. However, that was not enough reason to text her. Dereck knew she would text him if she was okay.

A week later, Jamaica began going to school. Again. She was always with Angelica but when he tries to join them, she runs away. What's her problem?

Angelica was also worried about Jamaica's actions. She knew based on her friend's behavior that she liked Dereck. Ever since they met, Jamaica liked him more than just a friend. She could see that Dereck didn't feel the same.

She never told her that. Knowing Jamaica, she was already aware of that fact. That Dereck only liked her as a friend.

Jamaica was welcomed by her daughter's kiss and warm embrace. "Mommy! You're finally home!" She hugged her tightly and then kissed the top of Camila's head. It scared her that if Dereck meets their daughter, he would take her away from her. "Mommy? Where's my chocolate?"

She released her and took the chocolate out of her bag. "Yehey!"

"Claire, I'll go home now," said Yaya Mel.

"Thank you, Yaya for taking care of Camila." She embraced the old woman who was like a second mother to her. "Take care."

"See you tomorrow." Yaya Mel caressed Camila's hair. "Bye, baby."

"Bye, Yaya." Camila hugged her in her thighs.

Camila already had a shower so she was just waiting for her mother on the bed. Minutes later, Jamaica stepped inside their room wearing a large yellow t-shirt and gray sweat-pants. She was drying her hair using a towel around her neck. "Baby, stop playing with your phone. You should rest your eyes now."

Being an obedient kid, Camila placed her phone on the bedside table and lay down on the bed. Jamaica sat beside her on the bed and asked a question. "Baby, do you want to meet Daddy?"

She stared at her mother for a long time. Jamaica was trying to read her daughter's face when she told her. "If you are not okay with that Mommy, I don't need to meet Daddy. It's okay to know that I have a Daddy."

Jamaica didn't know what to feel. How could her six-year-old daughter be more understanding than her? She wrapped her arms around Camila. "You are more than enough, Mommy." Tears began streaming down her face.

Camila wiped her tears. "Don't cry, Mommy. You'll be ugly if you cry."

Jamaica laughed at her daughter's sweetness. "Let's sleep now." She stood up to hang her towel behind the door and then climbed up the bed again. She covered herself and Camila with the blanket. Closing her eyes to sleep, she remembered the day when she and Dereck met.

Jamaica studied at Sofia University, an institution offering free tuition, free food, free uniform, and books. Even transportation for those students who could not enter other universities because of pricey costs.

The school offers education from preschool to college, and it was on a large hectare of land. Surrounded by trees, it had fresh air and was far away from pollution. The various departments were in separate buildings just across from each other.

She passed by the campus grounds near the Department of Performing Arts on her way to the Department of Medicine. Jamaica stopped for a while and watched a group of students cheering a group of dancers. She did not realize the time so when she glanced at her watch, she jumped in panic. "Oh no! I'm late for class!"

After their last subject, there was an orientation for freshmen students who wanted to join the theater club. Jamaica was a member of it and was in charge of the club's production set. She designed sets and props that the actors use.

She was behind the stage, sitting on the floor as she sketched some designs for the stage. Jamaica heard faint footsteps. Someone was coming in closer to where she was. "Hello?" It was the voice of a man. Then she heard the curtain open as he walked further. "Hello? Is anybody in here?"

Glancing up, her brown eyes instantly met her black ones. "Hi," she smiled at him, "are you a freshman?"

Dereck nodded and then sat beside her. "What are you doing?"

"Oh, I'm just sketching set designs." Jamaica continued drawing while he watched her. "What's your course, by the way?"

"I'm a first-year in Performing Arts majoring in Dance. You are?"

She didn't respond so Dereck grabbed her ID and read her name and course. "Ahh, Jamaica. What a nice name. You're a med student? How uncanny for you to be here."

"Why? Because it's different from the course that I took?"

"Yeah. I just find it weird."

Jamaica nodded, not bothered by what he said. And that was the beginning of their bittersweet friendship.

The following day, Angelica was waiting for Jamaica in the hospital's lobby. She immediately blocked her way when she saw her walking inside. "Why did you leave me at the dance school last night?"

"Sorry. I had to go home immediately."

"Why?" They stepped inside the elevator and Jamaica pressed the button to their department.

Jamaica couldn't tell that she had a daughter waiting for her because she knew once she told Angelica about Camila, Dereck would know it for sure. She changed the topic so Angelica didn't ask any further. "Sorry, I wasn't able to say goodbye. I was looking for you but you went missing."

"It's all right. I talked to my boyfriend to clear things up."

"What happened? Did you settle things between the two of you?"

Angelica smiled nevertheless, Jamaica could see the sadness in her eyes. "I don't know what's happening to us anymore. He said he never wanted to see me again."

"Did you do anything wrong?"

"That's what frustrates me. He's not telling me anything."

Jamaica could feel her. "I know you are not asking for any advice, Angel, I think you should give him up. He's not worth it."

"But-"

"I'm telling this because I care for you."

Angelica teared up and hugged her friend. "Thank you."

Jamaica stroked her back. "Remember, I'm always here for you."

Both of them got out of the elevator and headed to the changing room to wear their uniforms.

Dereck was sitting behind the desk and he was reviewing the profiles of the students who registered in the ballroom class. He was searching for Jamaica's file but he couldn't see it. He called Dave. "Hey, do you have the file of the woman with dark brown hair last night?"

"Who? The one who was with Angelica?"

"Yeah, that woman. Where is her file?"

"She didn't enroll in the class. Only Angelica." Dave told him. "Why? Do you want me to call Angelica and ask?"

"N-no. That won't be necessary." Dereck bit his lower lip. "Go back to what you were doing." Dave exited the room and went back to the information desk.

How will I meet her again? He thought. Will she come with Angelica to the next session?

Jamaica and Angelica were having coffee during lunch break when Angelica received a call. "Hello, Dereck? How unusual for you to call?"

Hearing his name coming out of her friend's lips, Jamaica clenched her jaws and looked away. The jealousy that she even shouldn't feel had been eating her up for seven years. She doesn't want to ruin her friendship with Angelica just because of him so she stayed quiet.

"Are you going to attend the next class?" He asked.

"Yeah, why?"

"I-I, uh, I just asked!" He said with a nervous laugh.

Angelica smirked as she glanced at Jamaica. She knew exactly why Dereck was asking her.

Chapter 4

Dereck was contemplating if he would call Angelica or not. He kept pacing back and forth inside the office until he finally dialed her number. "Hello, Angelica?"

"Hello, Dereck? How unusual for you to call?"

He cleared his throat and then casually asked if she would be coming back on Saturday for the next dance lesson. The truth was, he just wanted to know if Jamaica would join her but he couldn't ask it.

He's the great Dereck and girls ask about him not the other way around.

Saturday came and he prepared earlier before the class. He was in front of the mirror, fixing his hair and checking his outfit. He then headed to the dance school to wait for Angelica and Jamaica to come.

The class began but Jamaica was not there. He thought she would be dying to meet him again because that was the Jamaica he knew.

His only way now is to visit her in the hospital. And that was what he did.

"Hi, is Nurse Angelica around?" Dereck asked one of the nurses in the nurses' station.

"Oh, I think she's having lunch with Doc Jamaica and Doc Stephen. You can find them at the cafeteria."

"Thank you."

The cafeteria was huge. It was the whole floor. There was a coffee shop at the farther corner for those who wanted to drink coffee after a meal.

Dereck tried looking for Angelica until he spotted her sitting across from two doctors wearing coats. He instantly knew the other one was Jamaica.

He marched to their table. "Hey, Angelica!"

"Dereck? What are you doing here?"

Jamaica choked on her food upon hearing his name. She coughed hard.

"Are you okay, Claire?" The other doctor stroked her back and then handed her his glass of water.

"I'm fine."

Dereck was starting to get pissed. Ha! What a way for their public display of affection?! He scooted over Angelica's seat so she had to move over to the empty chair.

He rested his arms on the table and stared at Jamaica. However, she kept her head down avoiding his gaze.

"Why are you here, Dereck? You didn't even tell me you were coming." Angelica looked at him but his attention was only on Jamaica.

"I suddenly got curious."

"About what?"

"Why after all these years, she decided to come back now." He smirked.

Stephen was about to say something when Jamaica held his hand that was on top of the table. "Stephen..." Jamaica finally faced him. Her eyes were determined. "You don't have to tell anything to him."

Dereck glanced at their clasped hands. He had to close his eyes and breathe heavily. His whole body tensed. Standing up, he glared down at her and left.

She doesn't have any plan to explain to me why she left and why she came back? Ha! I don't care! I won't care anymore! He thought as he walked out of the cafeteria. "Tch."

"Are you okay, Jamaica?" Angelica asked when she noticed she was tearing up.

"I'm fine." She dried the tears in the corner of her eyes. How could I tell him if he acts like that? He didn't even mature just a bit. She looked at her friend and held her hands. "Angel, there is something I haven't told you yet."

Angelica only stared at her, waiting. "You don't have to tell me if you're not ready."

"I wanted to tell it to you when we met again but I didn't know where to begin."

"It's okay. Take your time."

Jamaica inhaled deeply and exhaled slowly. "I have a daughter."

"What? I think I did not hear you correctly."

"I. HAVE. A. DAUGHTER."

"What?! Who's the father?" Angelica stood up and then pointed at Stephen. He immediately raised his hands, shaking his head.

"He's someone you don't know." Jamaica stood to pull her down and sit again.

Angelica scoffed. She was literally annoyed. "You stopped all the communication because you got pregnant?"

"Sorry."

"I thought you and Dereck would end up together." She leaned on the chair and crossed her arms over her chest.

That's what I thought too. Jamaica answered in her mind.

"When will you tell it to Dereck?"

Jamaica was alarmed. "Huh?"

"When will you say it to Dereck? He also needs to know. We had been your friends since college. Don't you think he also had the right to know?"

The tension around them was interrupted when Stephen received a call. "Angge, we have a patient. Let's go."

The two left Jamaica with a lost appetite.

Stephen, followed by Angelica, reached the emergency room. "Doc Stephen, the patient is Rosette Morales, seventeen years old. She just had a seizure episode at home. Her mother said that it was her first time seeing her daughter have an attack. Her vitals are normal."

"Do a CT Scan, a MRI, and an EEG." The resident doctors followed his instruction then he waited for the results. He checked it on the computer.

Rosette was transferred to the pediatric ward and Stephen called her mother to his office. "Good afternoon, Mrs. Morales. Please have a seat."

"Thank you, Doc." Rowena settled down on the chair in front of Stephen's desk. "How's my daughter?"

"According to her laboratory results, she just had a seizure episode. It usually happens to people with epilepsy. Does your daughter have epilepsy?"

"Not that I know of." Mrs. Morales tried to remember anything that might be the cause. "During her childhood, even just a few days after giving birth, she had convulsions and was often sent to the hospital because of over fatigue. Is that related?"

"It might be, Ma'am. Let's get her admitted for other tests." Rowena agreed.

Rosette heard voices talking when she was finally conscious. She slowly opened her eyes and the first one she saw was the most handsome guy she had ever seen. His thick eyebrows pointed nose, chiseled jaw then he turned to her and stared. Oh my gosh! She wanted to scream. He's so handsome! She felt like she was being sucked in by his black orbs and his lips were inviting her.

"You're awake," the doctor checked her breathing using the stethoscope around his neck. She gasped at their proximity. I can't!

"Ms. Rosales. Your breathing is unstable. Are you okay?" He asked.

She could only nod and then hide her face behind the blanket.

"She's fine now. Just call me if she feels sick."

"Thank you, Doc Stephen.", Rowena said before watching the young doctor leave.

Stephen... Gosh, his name suits him.

Going back to his office, he passed by the vending machine where Jamaica was getting a cup of coffee. He decided to stop and have a chat with her. "Jamaica,"

"Hey, Doc Stephen." She looked around to see if there were other people around them. Others might start a rumor if they start to talk casually.

"Are you okay?"

"About what?"

"About what you told Angelica earlier."

"Yeah. I wanted to tell her even though it's late."

"Why didn't you tell him?"

"Who?"

"To Camila's father. Why didn't you tell him? He was that guy who came, right?"

"You knew?" Jamaica was surprised because she didn't tell Stephen anything about Dereck.

"I noticed it the moment he stared at you. He was like the splitting image of Camila."

"I planned to tell him. However, meeting him again and seeing that he hadn't changed made me scared. He might have a hard time accepting her. He might not be ready."

Stephen heaved a frustrated sigh. "Aren't you being too hard on him? I think you should talk to him properly. Give him the benefit of the doubt. If he's still like what you tell him he is, let Camila decide. After all, he's her father." He tapped her shoulder. "I'll go back to my office now. I'll send you home later so I can also visit Camila. I miss her already."

"Okay." She smiled watching him walk away. She suddenly remembered to ask for Dereck's number from Angelica.

Jamaica saw Angelica at the nurses' station and called her. "Angel, do you have Dereck's number?"

Angelica glanced at her but did not answer her question. She went to her and hugged her. "Sorry for not telling you soon and for missing for seven years. It was hard for me at that time."

The nurse pouted and she slowly turned to her. "You can tell me everything, Jam... Like how I can run to you, you can also do that. I'm always here for you."

"I know that."

"No secrets?"

Jamaica bit her lip and Angelica already knew there was something she wasn't telling yet.

"Jamaica?" She threatened. "You better tell me or else I won't talk to you anymore.

Scared of losing her friend, Jamaica grabbed her arm and dragged her to a quiet place. They entered the fire exit then Jamaica faced her. "Promise me you won't get surprised."

"That depends on what you're about to tell me. Come on, spill."

Jamaica nervously breathed out. It's Dereck."

"What about Dereck?"

"My daughter."

It took a few minutes for Angelica to realize what had just been told to her. Her eyes widened and her jaws dropped.

There was no voice coming out of her mouth. Jamaica closed her mouth, repeating what she said. "Dereck is the father of my daughter."

Her knees gave up on her. Luckily, Jamaica caught her in time and assisted her to sit on the stairs. She did not bother asking if Angelica was all right. It was visible to her that she was in too much shock.

"I didn't want to tell him because I think he did not even change."

"You didn't know what happened when you left." Angelica smiled bitterly. "I just couldn't tell you everything. I'll give you his number. I hope you can settle things. Don't become like me and my boyfriend." She took out her phone from her uniform's pocket and gave Dereck's contact information.

"Thanks." Jamaica embraced Angelica. "I'll give him a call so we can talk about our daughter."

"You still have to tell me what happened, okay?"

Jamaica smiled.

"And I want to meet my niece!" Angelica abruptly stood up. "I have to buy her gifts. What does she like? What is her favorite food? Toys?"

Jamaica laughed. "You can meet her later. Stephen will send me home to play with her."

"Okay. Let's stop at a pastry shop so I can buy her a cake. I'll go back to work now."

"I'll give Dereck a call."

"Do that."

Dialing his number, Jamaica placed the phone on her left ear and waited for him to answer. "Why isn't he answering?"

She tried to call him again, but still, there was no response. She received a text message that the other residents were looking for her so she went out of the fire exit and ran to the General Surgery Department.

She assisted in one of the surgeries. Since it was only a minor surgery it only took two hours to finish. Stepping out of the operating room, she decided to head to the cafeteria to buy coffee.

Jamaica reached the cafeteria and ordered an Iced Americano. She played on her phone while waiting for her order when someone stood beside her.

"What's your order, sir?"

"One Cookies and Cream Frappuccino and one Strawberry Frappuccino."

Wait, that voice sounds familiar. Jamaica instantly glanced over her shoulder and saw Dereck. Why is he back here in the hospital? Did Angelica tell him that I needed to talk to him? "Dereck, I-"

"Here's your order, Doc," the barista passed her drink to her.

"Thank you." She turned to Dereck again, "Dereck, do you have time? I need to talk to you."

"Sir, here are your orders." Dereck took the drinks from the barista and left Jamaica there.

She scoffed in disbelief. What the hell! Jamaica walked briskly to catch up to him until she saw him walk towards a certain table. A patient was sitting on a chair, smiling at him. "Yehey, strawberry!"

Dereck laughed. "Of course, that's your favorite and you're not allowed to drink coffee anymore."

"Hey, where did that come from?"

"I asked your mother what happened and she told me everything. I researched about it and you cannot drink any caffeinated drinks, okay?"

"Tch," the young lady crossed her arms over her chest and pouted. "Go home now. I can manage on my own."

Dereck laughed again and pinched her nose. "Silly, your mom told me to take care of you."

Jamaica couldn't take it anymore. She turned around and left. It's better to go home now. I need Camila.

Chapter 5

He ignored her on purpose. Again, to hurt her. To get even. Many might say he's childish because of what he's doing but he's hurt. He was hurt by the fact that Jamaica thought too little of him. She did not even tell him she would go away and she didn't even tell him she was back. What kind of friend is that?

How could she disregard our friendship just like that? He treated her even more than just a friend but what happened? He was ignored, so he promised himself that Jamaica would receive the same pain he felt.

He felt behind him that Jamaica was standing watching him and Rosette so he did what he used to do to her. He pinched Rosette's nose and joked.

Dereck also sensed that Jamaica walked away from them and left the cafeteria. His jaw tightened and he held his neck. An imaginary lump on his throat was so hard to swallow.

"Are you okay, Direk?"

"I'm fine." He smiled. "Do you want to go back to your ward?"

"Can we stay in the garden for a while? All the patients there are kids."

He laughed. "Of course, that's the pedia. You're still under-age so you're a pedia too. Once you turn eighteen, you'll be an adult then."

"I think I would still prefer to be a kid. I don't want to be an adult."

"Why? If you're an adult, you can do things you can't do if you're a kid."

"I don't want to be an adult if I were to become like you."

"Become like me? What's the problem with me?"

"I saw what happened earlier and I know what you were doing. I don't want to become like you who couldn't be true to himself."

"Ouch. Do you really see me like that?" He was hurt since it was the truth.

"Yeah." Rosette paused. "I saw from that doctor's face that she wanted to talk to you yet you didn't give her a chance."

"It was her fault. She disappeared for a long time then she'll come back just like that?"

"Tsk, tsk, tsk," She shook her head. "Did you just let the opportunity pass because of your hatred for her? I thought you were better than that, Direk."

He couldn't talk back to the kid. Everything she said was right.

"Don't waste your time and wait for the day when you'll regret what you've done."

Dereck assisted her. "Stop nagging. You're like my mother."

Rosette laughed. "Nah, I'm just a concerned citizen here. I can't afford to see the love life of my mentor go astray."

"Love life? Go astray?" He laughed so hard. "My relationship with her was hardly a love life."

"Really?" She grinned. "That's not how I see it. Anyway, whatever you say. Everything is up to you. I'm just stating my observation and my opinion."

Stephen parked his car in front of Jamaica's ancestral house. Camila ran outside welcoming them. "Mommy! Daddy Stephen!"

Jamaica opened the gate and received her daughter's warm embrace. "Did you have dinner, baby?"

"Yes, Mommy." She turned to the other visitor they had. "Who is she, Mommy?" Camila stared at Angelica for a long time.

It felt like she was looking at Dereck. A mini girl version of Dereck.

"Meet your Auntie Angelica. She's Mommy's friend."

"Nice to meet you, Aunt Angel."

"Nice to meet you, cutie." She held up the box of cakes. "Do you like chocolate cakes?"

Camila clapped while jumping up and down. That made them laugh.

"Let's go inside. Yaya Mel needs to go home."

Jamaica prepared the cake for the four of them while Stephen and Angelica played with Camila in the living room.

"Cutie, do you play with dolls?" Angelica asked. The kid nodded. "Do you want me to buy you one?" Camila only smiled.

"She already has dolls upstairs, Angel," Jamaica commented. She was holding two plates of cake and Stephen took it from her so she went back for the other two. They settled themselves on the floor.

They ate the cake as they watched Camila in her every movement. "Do you have her baby photos? I want to see it." Angelica asked.

"Yeah, I'll get it upstairs."

A moment later, Jamaica was back with a photo album and gave it to Angelica. It still surprised her to know that Dereck was the father. "What happened?"

Hearing that, Jamaica understood what she meant. "Stephen, can you wash Camila and put her to bed?"

"Sure." Stephen stood from the floor and carried Camila. "Come on, sweetie, let's go upstairs." The women watched them reach the second floor.

"Do you remember the time that I asked you to cover for me? That I slept over at your place?"

"Yeah."

"Dereck brought me to his father's wedding party. I accompanied him to a room and I didn't expect it would turn out like that."

"Is that why you suddenly avoided him? Why didn't you tell me?"

"You know how much I liked him, right? But he didn't feel the same and giving myself to him, I felt used. I was not thinking straight at that time. Especially when I discovered that I was pregnant."

"That's why you left?"

"I got scared that he would not take responsibility. That he would only be forced into a relationship he never wanted."

"Give him a chance now. There must be a reason why you met again. Because even if you both are in the same place, if God doesn't permit you to meet you won't see each other.

"I don't know if he'll talk to me again." He was ignoring me earlier.

"Just give him time. You know he just acts tough and cool but he's very sensitive. He didn't expect what you said earlier to him. He knew you as someone who would always take his side."

Jamaica nodded. "I'll do that. Let's talk about you. How did you meet your boyfriend?"

"Adrian is Dereck's roommate. When you left the three of us began going out. Until one day, he invited me out for dinner and asked if he could court me." Angelica sighed. "I told him to ask Dad's permission. He did that but Dad told him something then he started avoiding me."

"Do you have any idea what it might be?"

Angelica shook her head. "That's why I tried asking him when we went to the dance school. Nothing happened."

Jamaica held her hand. "Sorry I couldn't help you with anything."

"That's fine. I'm preparing myself. If the two of us are meant to be, God will make a way just like how you and

Dereck met again." Angelica looked her in the eye. "Take this as an opportunity for a chance. A second time around."

Dereck came back to the hospital the following day, carrying a basket of fruits for his student. He got inside the elevator and pressed a button when someone yelled. "Wait!"

He pressed the open button to let the other passenger in. "Thank you."

Both of them had surprised looks on their faces.

Jamaica cleared her throat and stood at the opposite end of the elevator. She hadn't pressed any button yet so he asked her. "What floor?"

"Huh?" Jamaica turned to her with a curious stare. "Ah, fifth floor." Dereck pressed it for her. "Thanks."

The door opened on the next floor and other passengers flooded in. They didn't have the chance to talk and he's thankful for that. He wanted to avoid confrontations because he was not good at expressing himself.

He hadn't noticed that she already exited the car. When he was in Rosette's ward, Dereck saw the doctor who was with Jamaica at the cafeteria. He frowned in annoyance even if the man wasn't doing anything.

"I'll tell you the results when your mother comes by later. So far, your vitals are stable. Take a lot of rest while you are here."

"Thank you, Doc Stephen." Rosette smiled at him and he smiled back.

Dereck was observing him so he was surprised when their gazes met. Stephen looked at him with anger in his eyes but he didn't know why. He cleared his throat looking away. He felt intimidated.

"I'll leave for now and check up on you later," Stephen told Rosette before giving Dereck one last look.

Sitting on the empty chair beside her bed, Dereck placed the basket of fruits down on the floor. "Why are you here again?" Rosette scrunched her face. "Why don't you manage your dance school well? This is the reason why there are no students. You're always outside."

Dereck flicked her forehead. "Why are you so disrespectful to your teacher?"

"Ouch!" She glared at him. "It's because you're annoying. Stop using me as your excuse to see her."

"Hey, I came here for you."

"Yeah, yeah. But the doctor said I'm fine." She shooed him away. "Talk to her. Don't come back here until you don't settle things with her. You are giving me a headache!"

"What did I do? When did I give you a headache, huh?"

"That!" She pointed to his face. "That look you had for the past few days. Please... spare me... I don't want to hear you saying you didn't do anything."

His nose flared and his teeth clenched. Thankfully, he doesn't fight kids. He knew Rosette was trying to get on his nerves because he was not doing anything. "Fine." He sighed. "You win." Dereck stood up. "I'll go talk to her."

When he went out of the ward, he thought of buying a drink at the coffee shop in the cafeteria. "Maybe I could buy one for her."

Unexpectedly, Dereck met Jamaica at the cafeteria. She was shocked to see him standing beside her. "D-Dereck. You're still here."

"Why? You didn't want to see me anymore?" He raised an eyebrow at her.

"No! No! It's not that." Jamaica licked her bottom lip and then bit it. She looked straight into his eyes and asked, "Can we talk?"

The two of them were sitting on one of the benches in the rooftop garden. Both of them were having their coffees. Jamaica was drinking an Americano while Dereck had a Cappuccino.

He glanced at the other drinks that were sitting in between them that he had to ask, "Why did you buy so much coffee?"

"I bought it for you. You might need it."

"Why?" He looked at her.

Jamaica breathed deeply before speaking. "I wanted to apologize. For what happened seven years ago."

His eyebrows knitted in confusion. He didn't say anything and waited for her to finish.

"Sorry for avoiding you without any explanation. Sorry for leaving and I'm sorry for ruining our friendship." She was playing with her fingers.

Dereck observed her. "There's only one way to save our friendship."

"Huh?"

"Give me the explanation you haven't told me."

Jamaica thought hard about how to tell it nicely without offending him. Here it goes! "It's because of what happened that night."

"Night?"

"When you brought me to your father's wedding party."

"What about that?"

She stared at him with wide eyes.

"Don't worry about that. Let's just forget about it. Is that the only reason why you avoided me and you didn't tell me you left?"

Jamaica realized it was not the right time to tell him about Camila. She nodded and did not bother to correct him. After all, it was just a one-night stand for him. She humorlessly laughed at the nonsense he was blabbering about. Luckily, her phone vibrated so she read the text. She had the chance to escape him. "Hey, they're looking for me now." She stood up. "Make sure to finish those coffees. See you some other time."

"Bye." Dereck waved. "Don't forget to attend the dance class with Angelica. See you then."

Jamaica nodded then ran away.

Watching her retreating figure, Dereck sadly smiled. He saw how burdened Jamaica was talking about what happened to them seven years ago. It looks like I have to gain her trust again.

Chapter 6

Adrian was having breakfast while checking his phone. "Why are you so focused on your phone?" Dereck came into the kitchen to get water from the refrigerator. He thought he was exchanging messages with his client but the truth was he was stalking Angelica on her social media page.

That's the only way he could know how she was doing. Ignoring and avoiding her was harder than he thought. However, Adrian was determined to show and prove to her father that he can be a worthy boyfriend for his daughter.

Being an orphan at an early age, it was not easy for Adrian to get to where he was. He had been working three part-time jobs while studying. He was thankful for Dereck because he assisted him in any way he could.

Dereck left home when he turned eighteen and they became roommates. He's also thankful for introducing Angelica to him. Though it was not his intention to fall in love with her. But the heart is truly a deceitful one. Only God knows what he feels.

She may misunderstand my actions right now. I'm hoping someday she will understand.

"How's your work?" Dereck asked.

"It's fine. I'm gaining experience and slowly I'm adjusting to the work. Why?"

"Can you still manage our dance school if you're busy?"

My hands are not really full. He thought. The problem is that my mind is occupied by Angelica most of the time. "I guess I can still help you."

"Are you sure? Because Angelica enrolled. And I know she did that to have a chance to have a conversation with you."

Adrian removed his glasses and massaged the bridge of his nose. "I can't tell her what her father told me." He put his glasses back on.

"Why? Is it because you're scared she'll break up with you?"

He couldn't answer. Dereck was right.

"Didn't it ever occur to you that avoiding her and simply ignoring her, your relationship is already going down the drain? Don't become like me. It took me seven years and right now we are not on good terms yet."

"Have you met Jamaica again?" Adrian paused. "How?" He had only heard Jamaica through Angelica. Dereck never mentioned her to him.

"How did you know her name?" Then Dereck realized. "Oh, Angel might be talking about her."

"Yeah." His mood suddenly changed. Hearing Angelica's name and talking about her had been exhausting his heart. It frustrated him that he couldn't do anything. Even if he tries to disobey her father, nothing will change. He was still someone who didn't deserve Angelica.

"She's working at the hospital where Angel is. I just don't have any idea in what department."

"What's your plan now?"

"Huh? What are you talking about?"

"Now that you two met again. What are you going to do? Are you going to pursue her now?"

"Pursue her? I don't even like her!" He adamantly denied then scoffed.

Adrian smirked. "Said by the man who had been mentioning her name almost every day for seven years." He finished eating his cereal and then went to the sink to wash the tableware he used.

"You don't believe me?"

"I didn't say that." He turned to face Dereck, smiling.

"I don't like her. I-I just missed her." Dereck looked away. Meeting Adrian's gaze, his eyes might say it all. He looked at him. "Hey, why are you making fun of me? Let's see if you can smile like Angelica knows the truth.

He searched for something to throw and saw a towel on the sink. Adrian threw it at Dereck's face. Bull's eye!

Dereck glared at him and then marched to his bedroom.

Rosette was discharged from the hospital so Dereck visited her. He was standing in front of a three-story building. The ground floor was a bar named Rowena's from her mother's name while the third floor was where their house was.

He went upstairs to the third floor and saw Rosette in the living room. She was watching a movie on the television. "How are you?"

She glanced at him then focused her attention on the TV. "I'm fine. You just visited me the other day at the hospital and now you're here again? Direk, you should really have a love life now."

"Even you?"

Rosette looked at him curiously.

"Adrian had been teasing me about Jamaica."

"It's because you keep on denying it."

He opened his mouth to argue but he closed it again since he already knew he wouldn't win. Even the kid could tell what he was feeling.

"Fine." Dereck sat on the couch. "Can you help me?"

"In what?"

"I wanted to know what she feels about me. If she still has feelings for me like before."

"Why do you need my help? Just ask her."

Dereck got annoyed. "It's not that easy. She's avoiding the topic."

"Really? Maybe she has someone else."

"Aren't you worried?"

"About what?"

"That someone else might be that doctor. Your crush."

"What?!" She suddenly sat up properly. "Doctor Stephen? That can't be! Direk, what can I do to help?"

He covered half of his face to hide his smile.

They planned on how to make Jamaica admit her true feelings.

Once again it was Saturday after work Angelica and Jamaica agreed to go straight to the dance school. Though she doesn't want to dance, Jamaica was determined to settle things between her and Dereck. If joining the class would help her fix her relationship with Dereck, she's fine with that. She would do anything for her daughter. To give Camila a complete family.

She wore the red flared dress and heels Angelica brought for her the other time. Looking at herself through the mirror, Jamaica noticed the dark circles under her eyes. "Girl, you look like a zombie.

Angelica was already dressed and also applied light make-up. "Let's put on some foundation to cover your dark circles and maybe fix your hair."

A few minutes later, Jamaica barely recognized herself. Her pale face glowed a little and the red lipstick helped in adding color to her lips. Her dark brown eyes were highlighted thanks to the eyeshadow Angelica used.

"That's better." Angelica felt proud of herself. "Aren't we both beautiful?" She smirked at her.

Both of them went inside the classroom. Upon their entry, Dereck was already standing in front and he was with the patient she saw in the hospital. What is she doing here?

They stood in the corner when Dereck started speaking. "Tonight, we will be joined by one of my theater dancers, Rosette. She will be helping in teaching the steps of Waltz."

Dereck and Rosette stood in their basic position and then settled their hands in the right places. Seeing it, Jamaica felt her blood boiling and her nose flaring in anger. She was surprised when Angelica whispered in her ear. "Relax, they're just dancing."

Jamaica turned to her friend as if she was caught in the act. Angelica chuckled. "You're so cute, Jamaica." She lightly pinched her cheeks.

Pouting, Jamaica removed Angelica's hand from her face.

"She's not looking at us. I guess she doesn't care." Rosette whispered to him while they were dancing.

Dereck tried to turn his head to look but she stopped him. "Don't. She might notice you are doing this on purpose. Later, take her as your partner, try to see her reactions."

He narrowed his eyes and looked at her with suspicion. "Are you sure of what you're saying? What if she gets mad?"

"Hmmm... I don't think so."

They finished showing the dance so he told the students. "Now, find a partner or your partners from the last session and we'll try to do it simultaneously."

The other students had partners but Angelica and Jamaica did not have one. Dereck grabbed Jamaica's hand and pulled her towards him. All of a sudden, Adrian came. "Hey, Adrian, come here. Angelica doesn't have a partner yet."

Adrian glared at him.

"Come on, Adrian, the others are waiting." Rosette finally said. He took off his suit jacket and folded his sleeve up to his arms. He avoided meeting Angelica's eyes but he held out his hand. She grabbed it and they stood properly.

"Are you ready? Remember the hand positions." Dereck told the students. He placed Jamaica's left hand on his right arm then he held her right hand with his left hand. He glanced at Rosette and she played the song.

Jamaica was surprised to hear the song So Close by John Mclaughlin. It was her favorite song. Because of that, she immediately looked up at Dereck and saw him wiggling his eyebrows.

They were dancing but it was different unlike when he was teaching her the first time. Now, it was with an unexplainable feeling. She could catch up to his long strides without any hassle. Jamaica was beginning to enjoy the moment.

Meeting his gaze, she gave him her most sincere smile.

Seeing her smile like that, his heart skipped a beat. Wait, this is not part of my plan! I'm supposed to be doing it. Not the other way around!

Dereck had to look away. Staring at her too much felt like he would melt. She didn't have this effect on me before. What is happening? He glanced at Rosette who was enjoying themself as she watched them. The kid gave him a thumbs up.

He turned to Jamaica again and his heartbeat became faster and louder. I hope she doesn't hear it. His gaze moved to her red lips and made him gulp. He wanted to taste those inviting lips of her and remember how he savored them once.

Thankfully the song had finally come to an end. Without saying anything, he marched out of the room and headed straight to his office to have a cold drink.

Jamaica got curious about his action. When she glanced in Angelica's direction, she caught the two were standing awkwardly beside each other. Adrian grabbed his jacket, sat on a chair and followed Dereck outside.

Rosette took over and told them. "That's Waltz. If you want to practice, we still have a few minutes before the class ends. After that, you can go home. Thank you." Then she ran after the two.

Jamaica took that chance to approach Angelica. "Hey, are you okay?"

"Yeah. I'm just not used to it when he's ignoring me. Adrian is a really sweet guy. He's not usually like that." Jamaica patted her shoulder.

"Just wait for the right time. One day, he'll talk to you."

"I hope I can be patient enough to wait for that day."

Inside the office, Rosette saw Dereck drinking from a bottle of water and Adrian was fanning himself using his shirt. "What are you two doing?"

The men looked at her. "The plan didn't work out.", Dereck said.

Adrian on the other hand pushed his glasses on the bridge of his nose. "What plan are you talking about?"

"Really? What was her reaction like?" Rosette asked. She wanted details. Because if Dereck and Jamaica's relationship progresses she won't have any rivals against Doctor Stephen.

"Uh-" He couldn't utter a word to describe it. Dereck sighed in frustration.

Their conversation was halted when they heard a car parked in front of the building. Since the office was the first room you entered, Dereck immediately saw through the window who the person was outside.

It was none other than Stephen. "What is he doing here?" He muttered under his breath.

"Who?" Rosette went to the window and had a peek.

"Your doctor." Dereck's mood went sour as he stepped away from the window and finished his remaining drink.

"I'll welcome him." She ran outside to meet Stephen.

Excited to see her crush, Rosette was smiling ear to ear when she greeted the doctor. "Hello, Doctor Stephen! What are you doing here?"

"Hi, Rosette, I didn't expect to meet you here."

"I know the owner and I take dance lessons here."

"Oh, so you dance, huh?" She nodded. "Anyway, I came here to get Nurse Angelica and Doc Jamaica. Can you call them for me? They said the lesson was about to finish so I came a bit early."

"Oh," Rosette's smile faded. It immediately turned into a frown. "Just wait here, I'll go upstairs and call them."

A minute later the two women were going down the stairs still dressed in their ballroom uniforms.

"Wow! You look fabulous!" The doctor commented.

Rosette could see that Stephen's eyes were glued on Jamaica. What is this feeling? She thought. It was her first time experiencing it and she didn't like it.

Chapter 7

Stephen received a text message from Angelica telling him to pick Jamaica up from the dance school since she can't drive her home.

Since he was heading home, he decided to go to the address Angelica sent.

The place was only thirty minutes away from the hospital because it was past rush hour. He parked his blue SUV in front of the building she described in her message.

He turned off the engine and got out of the driver's seat. Stephen quietly made his way to the entrance. He was surprised to see one of his patients opening the door for him. "Hello, Doctor Stephen! What are you doing here?"

"Hi, Rosette, fancy meeting you here." Stephen looked around. They were standing in the hallway. There were stairs at the end leading to the second floor.

"I know the owner and I take dance lessons here."

"Oh, so you dance, huh?" That's nice. She's pretty and looks like a great dancer. "Anyway, I came here to get Nurse

Angelica and Doc Jamaica. Can you call them for me? They said the lesson was about to finish so I came a bit early."

"Oh, just wait here, I'll go upstairs and call them."

Rosette came down later and told him, "They'll be coming down in a minute."

Just after that, he saw the lady he was waiting for. They were still dressed in their ballroom uniforms coming down the stairs elegantly. "Wow! You look fabulous!" His eyes were glued to Jamaica.

Few were the moments he had seen her dress up for any occasion so it was somewhat refreshing to see her in that outfit.

"Right, Doc?" Angelica smirked. "It's nice to dress up once in a while." She turned around gracefully.

"Yeah. We are too busy in the hospital so it's nice to do other activities like this. Sadly you didn't invite me."

Peeking through the closed blinds, Adrian saw Angelica's smile for the first time since he started ignoring her. It hurt him to see her sad and he wanted to punch himself for that. If he was only a bit worthy of her then maybe there wouldn't be any problem. He glanced at the man who arrived and saw he was handsome enough for Angelica to like.

He knew she had a weakness for good looks. Angelica always told her she has a crush on any handsome guy she met.

And now he's starting to worry. He turned around and pretended to not see them. Maybe that's for the best. If she finds someone else, I'll accept it, he thought but his heart had a different opinion.

"We'll be going now," Angelica told Rosette.

"Come to the hospital for your checkups, okay?" Stephen reminded her patient.

Adrian saw Rosette smile and guide the three outside. He was then able to relax and breathe comfortably. The pain he was feeling might not be seen but it was slowly destroying him emotionally.

Rosette entered the office with a sour face. She sighed and plopped her body on the couch.

Looking at everyone in the room, he thought, do we have the same problem here?

"I'll be going home now," Angelica told the two when they were outside the building.

"Why did you call Stephen? You even disturbed him." Jamaica said.

"I had my reasons." Angelica smiled at her accomplishment. "Doc, make sure you send my friend home safe and sound, alright?"

Stephen saluted at Angelica then the three of them separated. "See you tomorrow."

"Bye!" Angelica started her car's engine and drove off.

"Get in," he opened the door for Jamaica and then ran to the driver's seat. He got in and buckled Jamaica's seatbelt before doing his.

"Thanks." She smiled and he did the same.

Meanwhile, the other three agreed to have dinner in a nearby restaurant. They were silently eating as if life had turned its back on them. Rosette had been thinking of what she witnessed earlier. Recalling Jamaica's appearance she admitted she doesn't stand a chance.

How will I get Doc Stephen's attention? She stared at Dereck who was only looking down at his food. What should I do to help Direk get Doc Jamaica's heart? She was getting frustrated so she filled her mouth with food.

Choking, she coughed so hard. "Hey, why are you eating so fast?" Adrian handed her a glass of water.

She really doesn't like what she's feeling.

The following day, Rosette went to the hospital's pharmacy to buy her medicines since they can only be bought there.

Thankfully, the pharmacy was at the left corner of the lobby. "Hi, I'm here to buy my meds. Here is the prescription."

Rosette waited for the pharmacist to give her medicines when someone tapped her lightly on the shoulder. She immediately turned and was astonished to see it was her favorite doctor. "Doc Stephen, good morning."

"Good morning," he flashed his most charming smile, "are you buying the medicines I prescribed you?"

She nodded, then the pharmacist called her. "Here are your medicines."

Rosette turned to get it and pay for it. She looked back at Stephen. "Do you want to have a drink? I'll treat you to a non-caffeinated one."

The two went to the cafeteria where the coffee shop was. Stephen asked her. "What would you like to have?"

"Hmm... I'd like to drink Hot Chocolate."

"Okay." He turned to the barista, "Two Hot Chocolate, please."

When their drinks were handed to them, Stephen invited her to the rooftop garden. They were sitting side by side on a bench, feeling the early morning breeze.

"It's nice that today's not too hot." He said.

"Yeah. I could enjoy a walk before going home."

"By the way, I just want to ask if you don't mind, are you not studying right now?"

"Oh, I'm not. After finishing senior high school, I started helping at my mother's restaurant and at the same time worked three to four part-time jobs."

Stephen frowned. "That's why you had a seizure attack.

Rosette smiled, biting her lower lip. "I just really overwork myself, sometimes I get sent to the hospital because of over-fatigue." His eyebrows knitted even more.

"Tch." Stephen took a sip of his sweet drink. "Anyway, how did you meet him?"

"Who?"

"The man who was visiting you when you were confined here."

"Oh, you mean Direk? He's a theater director and he scouted me when he saw me performing on stage."

"You were dancing?"

Rosette leaned closer and smiled from ear to ear. "No, I was singing." Both of them laughed.

"Really?"

"Yes! One day, you'll get to hear me sing. And dance. And maybe act."

"I'll be waiting for that. Make sure to invite me, okay?"

She smiled and simply stared at him. "Doctor Jamaica... Do you like her?"

Stephen choked on his drink. "Is it that obvious?"

Rosette nodded. "The way you look at her says it all." She was jealous but she didn't show it. "How did you meet her? And what do you like about her?"

Smirking, Stephen asked, "Is this a sort of interview?"

She shrugged her shoulders. "You can call it any way you want."

He tilted his head and looked up, thinking. "Hmm... I met her during the most difficult days of her life. Even though everything was hard for her she was strong and brave to face it head-on."

She had to look away. Never did she imagine liking someone who likes someone else would be this hard.

Instead of giving any comment Rosette quietly drank her hot chocolate not feeling the burning sensation in her tongue. It was the most bitter drink she had. She changed the topic. "If you have time you could visit our restaurant, Doc. We have live jamming sessions every Friday."

"Okay, as long as I don't have scheduled surgeries during that time."

She smiled in return. "I'll head home now. I still have to help in the resto."

"Sure, I'll see you off."

"No need. See you some other time."

Leaving him, Rosette threw the drink in the nearest trash bin she could find. Hot Chocolate was now removed from her favorite list of drinks.

It was Jamaica's day off. Luckily it was a Sunday. She could bring Camila to the mall and watch a movie on a big screen. Since she was at home, Yaya Mel was not around.

She got up, said a little prayer, and headed downstairs to prepare their first meal of the day.

Opening the fridge, she looked for all the ingredients she was about to use. She picked some processed meats, green peas, and carrots to make mixed rice. It was the easiest and fastest meal to prepare for her.

It was already ten in the morning when she woke up. Thankfully, Camila was still asleep. She could take her time cooking and at the same time relax.

Jamaica walked to the living room and grabbed a remote control. It was for the sound player. She turned it on and chose her favorite songs to be played.

She began singing and dancing along to the songs of Steps, the British pop group formed in 1997. She did not notice her daughter go down the stairs and watch her from afar. Camila's mouth parted in shock. She was only noticed by her mother when she took the remote on top of the coffee table and stopped the player.

"Huh? Why did it stop?" Jamaica went back to the living room. "Sweetheart, did you turn it off?"

Camila nodded. "You dance weird, Mommy."

Jamaica had to laugh it off. "Oh my gosh," I can't believe she's like her father, she thought.

"Why are you laughing, Mommy?" She cutely frowned at her.

Taking her daughter in her arms, she hugged Camila tightly and then tickled her. The little kid laughed so hard, still, it was music to her ears. "Do you want to go to the mall today and watch a movie?"

Camila's eyes gleamed brightly and smiled.

"Let's eat breakfast then I'll bathe you." They walked to the kitchen and had a hearty meal.

Carrying Camila in her arms, Jamaica reached the bus stop. They waited for an airconditioned and uncrowded bus to ride. Both of them were settled in their seats, Camila was the one sitting by the window when she asked, "Mommy, why don't we have a car like Daddy Stephen?"

"It's because Mommy can't drive."

"Really?"

Jamaica pinched her daughter's nose. She knew how to drive but because of an accident, she got scared holding the steering wheel again. It was one moment in her life she wanted to forget.

The conductor called all the passengers who needs to go down to the bus stop and they were one of them. "Come on, sweetheart. We still have to walk to the mall."

When they got down, Jamaica wanted to let Camila walk but there were too many people in that place so she carried her again. The kid was almost seven years old and she was very heavy. However, she feared losing her in that big city. She'd rather have a hard time because that's what mothers do. And that was what she realized when she became one.

Inside the mall, she put her down and held her right hand firmly. It was not Camila's first time in a mall, still, it fascinates her to see a lot of things. She started pointing to anything she was interested in. "Mommy, Mommy, let's go there." Her daughter kept on pulling her.

"Wait, sweetheart," Jamaica stood still then held her on the shoulders. "Where do you want to go? Just choose one. Do you want to eat or do you want to watch a movie first?"

"Eat first!"

"Alright." She grabbed her hand again and they walked side by side to the restaurant she was pointing to. Jamaica did not notice Dereck stepped inside the building and passed by them.

At the restaurant, Jamaica stood in line with her daughter. "What do you want to eat?"

Camila was looking at the digital menu board searching for the food she wanted. "I want chicken! And fries! And ice cream." That's what they ordered. She didn't order something for her because she knew her daughter won't be able to finish it.

After the meal, they headed to the cinema on the upper floor of the mall. "Jamaica, is that you?" Dereck was looking at her and Camila. Oh no!

Chapter 8

Dereck wanted to relax and take his mind off of some things. No Jamaica for today. She had been running through his mind since last night and he was really tired of thinking about her. Ever since their dance during the class, his heart had not been beating the same way that it was.

When he's in the mall, he takes his time roaming around looking for something or anything that could be an inspiration for him to write new scripts for a play.

He looked up and saw the posters of the movies that were showing in the cinema. "Maybe I could watch a few." He rode the escalator to the top floor and because it was the weekend there were many people, especially families who went out to bond and have fun.

Looking at them, he was really envious. He did not have any memories of being with both his father and mother even when she was still alive. He once dreamed of experiencing it. Maybe now with his own family. One day.

He was standing among the crowd waiting for the ongoing movie to finish when his eyes fixed on a very familiar figure. "Is she also here to watch a movie?"

Slowly he took his steps and approached her. "Jamaica, is that you?" He did not say that she was with someone else until she spoke.

"Hey, Mister, do you know my Mommy?"

Dereck averted his gaze to the kid Jamaica was holding. "Who is this kid? Is she your niece?"

She bit her lower lip and averted her gaze.

He tried to look her in the eyes. "Why? Is she your friend's daughter?"

Jamaica lowered her head and whispered, "She's our daughter." He still heard it.

"What? Our..." Dereck glanced at the kid again. He was taken aback. He instantly knew the moment he laid his eyes on her that the kid was his. His lips parted but he couldn't utter a single word. His jaws clenched and his hands balled into fists trying to control the anger within him. With knitted eyebrows, he looked at Jamaica with hurt in his eyes.

"Dereck, I can explain..." He could see how nervous she was. Her voice and hands were trembling. All of sudden, loud laughter escaped his lips. He laughed so hard. One he never had in a while. It was the funniest joke he had ever heard. His laughter caught the attention of other people around them so he slowly calmed himself.

He turned around, not wanting to say hurtful words. I have to get out of here.

He felt suffocated. And that was what he did. He ran away. His hands on his chest, his strides grew bigger just to immediately get out of that place.

Yes, it was one of his wishes. But he didn't want it to happen like that.

Wandering around the streets, he remembered their first night. A frown formed on his face. We just did it once and... we have a cute daughter?! Why didn't she tell me?! He pulled his hair out in frustration. Wait, the kid might not be mine. I have to make sure first.

Jamaica and Camila were inside the cinema. All seats were occupied and people were busy laughing their hearts out. She glanced at her daughter who was giggling too. Thankfully she's not asking anything or I won't be able to answer her nor make her understand. She felt like crying but she couldn't show it to Camila. Her heart was very heavy remembering the look on Dereck's face.

Even though the cinema was so cold, she couldn't breathe. She was sweating a lot. She knew it was her fault for not telling him. Jamaica just didn't expect it was more painful he treated her like she was a stranger. Because of the look in his eyes.

Looking at the phone in her hand, she contemplated if she would call Dereck or not.

After watching the movie Jamaica brought Camila to the play area. The little girl ran to the slide and she watched her enjoy it. Still, she was distracted by what happened. "Should I call him or not? She whispered to herself. Her eyes had been shifting to Camila and then back to her phone.

She walked to her daughter and asked, "Sweetheart, do you want to eat? Then we'll go home."

Camila smiled and nodded.

After finishing their afternoon activity, the mother and daughter rode on the bus to get home. Their travel time took almost three hours until Jamaica was able to get off their stop. Camila fell asleep along the trip so she carried her as she walked to their house.

She saw Stephen's car waiting in front of the house. He got out of the driver's seat and greeted her. "Claire!" Stephen waved his hand.

He helped her open the gate and the front door then both of them entered the house.

Jamaica put Camila on the bed while Stephen waited for her in the living room. her daughter from Dereck and watched him leave.

She was going downstairs when he asked, "How's your mother and daughter bonding? You didn't even invite me."

"Camila's father saw us."

"It was the man at the dance school, right? So... what did he say?" He sat again on the sofa across Jamaica.

Jamaica's shoulders fell. "He laughed when I told him. Maybe he couldn't believe what I just said."

"Still, he should've listened to what you had to say."

"I knew he would react like that. I expected that already it was just too sudden to meet like that."

"Have you told your parents about it?"

She only shook her head. "I'll tell them some other time."

"Okay." He nodded his head. "If there's anything I can help you with, don't hesitate to let me know. I'll go now." Stephen stood up and headed to the door. "You don't have to show me out. I'll lock the gate."

"Goodnight, Stephen." She gave him a reassuring smile.

"Goodnight, Claire. See you tomorrow." Looks like I have to make an extra effort if I want her to see my efforts.

Opening their apartment door, Dereck was welcomed by his roommate. "Did you have dinner?" Adrian was having his meal at the dining table.

"Not yet." He couldn't eat after his encounter with Jamaica.

Adrian handed him a glass of cold water. "Here you go. It looked like you needed a drink."

He gladly took it and had a sip. "Oh, before I forget. Do you know any private investigators?"

"Hmm... yes, why? Do you need to investigate someone? Who is it?"

"It's Jamaica. Turns out we have a daughter."

"Oh shi-" Adrian closed his mouth. He never swears but hearing shocking news made him slip his tongue. He cleared his throat and fixed his glasses. "Why do you need a private investigator?"

"I still cannot believe that the kid is mine."

"You don't believe in Jamaica?" Seeing that he couldn't answer, Adrian immediately knew. "Okay, I'll talk to a friend of mine and then give you an update."

"Thanks." Dereck entered his room and plopped down on his bed. He stared at the ceiling and kept thinking, Where did everything go wrong? How could she hide our daughter from me? Why?

During their breakfast, Alexander Garcia, Angelica's father, told her. "Darling, I have set a blind date for you. I'll text you the address and the name of your blind date. Make sure you dress properly and prepare for that."

"Dad," Angelica knitted her eyebrows. "I don't want to attend that."

"What do you want to do? To date that lawyer who did not even ask my permission to court you?"

"But Dad, I like him."

"Yes you like him, but where is he now? Why don't I see him? He told me he feels the same way for you."

"H-he's avoiding me..." Angelica looked away from her father's stare.

"And why is that?" She also did not know. "If his intentions are true, he would do everything to show his efforts to give you the reassurance that what the two of you have is real."

She wanted to cry. She stood up from her seat. "You still need to go to the blind date I mentioned. I am not accepting "no" as an answer."

Without finishing her meal, Angelica headed out. She'd rather be in the hospital and kill herself from overworking than think.

She busied herself as soon as she arrived at the hospital. Angelica only stopped for a quick break and that was when Jamaica spotted her in the rooftop garden having a cup of coffee.

"Hey, Angel, I've been looking for you."

"Oh, I was a bit busy." She didn't want to tell Jamaica any more of her problems. Angelica knew she was already troubled by many things.

"You don't have to tell me if you don't want to. I'm here when you're ready." Jamaica looked up at the sky and smiled. "The truth is, I was looking for you."

"Huh? Why?"

"I need someone to talk to." She turned to her. "A friend who would listen and understand."

"Awww... Jamaica!" Angelica hugged her tight. "What is it?"

"Dereck saw me with Camila at the mall yesterday."

"You mean he knows about his daughter?"

Jamaica nodded her head. "I told him I will tell everything some other time but I don't know where to start."

"Just tell him how you really feel. And after that, if he doesn't accept Camila you don't have any liability."

"Why is it so hard?"

"Do you know why?" Angelica asked her.

Jamaica only shook her head.

"It's because we're not letting Him lead us. We are not letting Him do what He wants to do for us when we cannot even do things by ourselves. She chuckled. "Funny, right? I know what to do? To let God rule our lives. Still, I'm stubborn and I wanted to do things my way, that's why I'm hurting."

"Angel..." The resident doctor held her hand and looked at her with much concern.

"Don't worry about me, Jamaica. From now on, I'll let Him do the best for me." For the first time in a while, she smiled happily. She thought that everyone had problems and might have been having a tougher battle than hers. How could this kind of relationship get me depressed? It's not worth it.

Angelica did not mention her blind date to Jamaica. From now on, I'll be strong with God's help and be strong for the people I love.

After her shift, she went to a boutique to buy a dress for her appointment.

Standing in front of a full-length mirror, Angelica mixed and matched clothes that suited her best until she wore a cobalt blue one-piece off-shoulder dress and white sling-backs shoes. She complimented it with an olive-colored clutch bag.

Satisfied with her overall outfit, she swiped it with her card and went off to her blind date.

She arrived at a fancy five-star restaurant where her father arranged the date. The glass door was opened by the host for her. "Good evening Ma'am, do you have any reservations?"

"Yes. Under the name Mr. Alexander Garcia."

The host checked the records and then guided her to the table. "This way, Ma'am."

Reaching her table, Angelica immediately approached her date. "Are you Mr. Henry Garcia?"

The guy was wearing an all-black attire from his baseball cap, and glasses to his running shoes. He looked up and gave her a small smile. "Yes, are you Ms. Angelica Garcia?" Henry stood up and offered a handshake.

Angelica gladly took it. "Sorry, I'm late."

"No, that's fine." He pulled a chair for her. "I was a bit early. Do you want to order now?"

"Sure." He seems nice, she thought. Henry called the waiter to order. A man came to their table and handed them the menu. "What would you like to have, Angelica?"

She glanced up from looking at the menu. She was surprised to hear him say her name. "Is it okay if I call you Angelica?"

"Yeah." She cleared her throat. "I'd like a Beurre noisette."

"A Grilled Lamb Chops for me. And for the drinks, a bottle of red wine."

"Okay, sir. I'll be right back." The waiter left with their orders and then came back with glasses of water.

"So, Angelica, I heard you are a nurse. What made you take that path? Your father is a lawyer, I thought you'll follow in his footsteps."

"Well, after my mother died, I wanted to learn how to take care of others. It was something I wasn't able to do for my mom. How about you?" She instantly felt comfortable around him so she didn't have any problem telling something personal to him.

"Me? I'm the Marketing Department Head at ZBS but my grandfather wants me to take over his position. I'm not ready for that and I couldn't see myself there. That's why he's been bugging me to attend blind dates and get married instead." He answered, shaking his head with a smile on his face.

Their orders came so they both turned to the server. What shocked Angelica was the man who passed behind the server. Adrian was with a woman smiling. What is she doing here? And with a beautiful woman at that?

Adrian turned in her direction and their eyes met. His expression suddenly changed.

Chapter 9

He had dinner with a client in a fancy restaurant. Being a lawyer had its perks and benefits, and that's why he chose it. However, he still needs experience if his goal is to make his name known and establish his very own firm.

Adrian was making his way out of the place with the client when they passed by a table where a waiter was serving meals. To pass by without any mishaps, he looked down and watched his steps. But by the time he lifted his head, his eyes unconsciously glanced to his side and saw someone familiar at one table.

He squinted his eyes and looked through his glasses. Adrian saw Angelica was having dinner with a man he doesn't know. Who's that guy?

All of a sudden, Angelica turned to where he was standing. Their eyes met but she avoided his gaze and pretended she did not see him. Ouch! He sadly left the restaurant.

"Hey Adrian, are you okay? Do you know that woman?"

"Huh?" He shook his head. "No, I don't know her."

The client shrugged her shoulders. "Anyway, I'll go now. Thank you for your assistance. I'll just contact you again."

"I'm home." Adrian stepped inside the apartment and closed the door.

"Hey, did you have dinner?" Dereck asked from the kitchen. He was watching basketball on the television.

"Yeah, I met a client and we ate together." He dragged his feet to the living room and plopped his body on the sofa. "I'm so tired. Do we have a beer?"

"Cola only, dude." Dereck chuckled. "You know we don't drink. Why do you want to get drunk?" He stood up and took two solo bottles of cola out of the fridge. He handed over one to Adrian. "Here you go."

Without saying anything, Adrian opened the bottle and finished it in seconds.

"Spill. What is it?"

"I saw Angelica having dinner with some guy."

Dereck sat beside him. "What do you want to do now?"

"The truth is I don't know what to do. I just want to get away from here and clear my mind."

"It's your call, dude. Even if I suggest anything, the final decision will still be yours."

Adrian placed his right arm on his eyes and thought hard. He had been pondering for a few days if he'll leave or not.

"I received an invitation from a college classmate to work in Australia."

"Really?"

He nodded. "I think this is the perfect opportunity to gain more experience and upskill."

"What about her? Are you good at leaving her?" Adrian inhaled deeply and loudly blew out his breath. He did not answer him, instead, he stood up and went straight to his room.

Dereck shook his head. He was worried for his friend though he had his problem to take care of.

Adrian peeked through his door and said, "By the way, I already contacted a private investigator. I'll give his contact information to you."

"Thanks, dude. Just text it to me."

Inside his bedroom, Adrian removed his suit and long-sleeved polo. He laid down on the bed staring at the ceiling as he vividly recalled how he first met Angelica. And how meeting her changed his whole life.

It was in early 2010 when Angelica was just nineteen years old. She was already in her fourth year in nursing and an intern in a general hospital.

He, on the other hand, was reviewing for the bar exam and at the same time working two part-time jobs just to make ends meet.

One day, he was sent to the emergency room because of over-fatigue. Adrian woke up after sleeping for almost five hours. His eyes slowly opened and the first person he saw was Angelica.

She was adjusting the IV drip flow rate and then glanced at him. "Are you awake now?"

"What happened?"

"You passed out."

He panicked. "What time is it?"

Angelica checked her wristwatch. "It's 6:30 p.m."

Adrian removed the needle on the back of his hand. "I need to go to work now or I'll be late. Where can I settle my bill?" She watched him with amusement in her eyes. Her lips were curving into a smile.

He looked at her curiously, "Why?"

She only shook her head. "I'll take you there." He walked behind her and observed her. He was smitten by her beautiful smile.

Adrian turned to his side and closed his eyes to sleep remembering the sweetest memory he had of her.

One week passed and Dereck met with the private investigator. They met at a coffee shop near the dance school. The investigator was around his late 30s or early 40s. "Here's what you've been asking for." He handed him a brown envelope.

Dereck opened it and read the data from the paper. "Seven years ago, she and her family went to Canada after discovering she was pregnant. She continued her studies after three years at a state university. During her pregnancy, she met a doctor named Stephen Brown, the son of the CEO of the hospital where she's working right now. There's a picture of her daughter inside." The PI said before drinking his coffee.

Looking at the picture, he saw his and the kid's similarities.

"I think you don't have to doubt if you're the father. It's so obvious that even I can tell. If you're okay with that, I'll get going. Just send the payment to my account."

He already knew that the moment the investigator told him why Jamaica left. Still, he needed evidence; proof that everything was true.

Jamaica had been waiting for him to call or text her because she knew he would do that if he was ready. But waiting was not Jamaica's cup of tea anymore. She wanted to settle things with Dereck once and for all, especially now that he met their daughter.

She dialed his number and waited for her call to connect.

"Hello?" He answered! "Why did you call?" Dereck sounded uninterested.

"I-Can we meet?"

"Fine. Let's talk."

Jamaica arrived at the coffee shop and saw him seated at one far corner. He was drinking frappe when his eyes were on her.

She awkwardly approached him and sat on the chair across from him. "Hi!"

He just stared at her with a blank expression. Dereck checked the time on his wristwatch. "I hired a private investigator because I don't believe she's mine."

Did I hear it right? Did he hire an investigator? She looked at him with unexplainable irritation. I thought he was just a jerk but he's a total pain in the ass. Jamaica fisted her hands in annoyance. She was offended because she never wanted everything that had happened. Why does it feel like everything is my fault now? If I only knew he's like this I never would've told him. I thought I knew him. I was wrong.

Dereck continued babbling nonsense. "I still don't believe she's mine after reading this." He held up the envelope given by the investigator.

She couldn't stand it anymore. Jamaica smashed her fists on the table and stood up. She glared at him and took out a small plastic pouch. "Use this all you want and ask for a paternity test." The pouch contained Camila's hair samples.

With that, she left him. She held her head up high. She will never regret having Camila in her life. If he doesn't accept her, fine! He can't blame me for not telling him.

He had never seen Jamaica get mad. It was new for him. A new side of her. Instead of being angry, he found it... interesting. A smile crept on his handsome face. All the ill-feeling he had melted away the minute he saw her walking inside. He placed a hand on his chest and double-checked his feelings. What does she really mean to me?

Not wanting to waste time, he called Rosette to ask for help in looking for a DNA testing facility. "Is it for you Direk?"

"Yup."

"Why?"

"Surprisingly, I have a daughter. But I'm not sure if she's mine."

"You and Jamaica have a daughter? Wow! Can I see a picture?" Dereck sent the picture to Rosette. "You know what, Direk? You don't have to do a paternity test. Anyone could tell that she's yours."

He did not say anything. "Just look for one."

"Okay. I've got to go now. I still need to study. Bye."

"Bye."

Arriving at the hospital hours earlier before her shift, Jamaica went straight to the coffee shop at the cafeteria to order the coldest drink available. "Can you please add more ice?"

The barista made her request. "Here you go."

"Thanks." She said before going to the rooftop garden. She searched for the most hidden place and screamed in a controlled voice. Breathless, Jamaica sipped on the drink she bought.

"Hey, Jam, are you okay?" Angel popped her head out from the side scaring her. "I followed you here because I noticed you look annoyed. Is there a problem?"

Jamaica sipped again then replied, "I'll be fine." She glanced at Angelica and smiled. She knew her friend wouldn't buy it. "I met with Dereck and he told me he did not believe Camila is his daughter so he hired a private investigator."

"What?! Why did he have to do that when he could've asked you instead?"

"That's why I'm angry. He needed more solid proof so I gave him Camila's hair samples he could use for the paternity test. I don't care if he will use it or not. I'll stop here. He already knows and it's up to him." Jamaica had a sip of her drink again. "It really irritates me when I remember the look on his face. I wanted to punch him!"

"Calm down, do you want me to talk to him?"

Hearing Angelica say that Jamaica did not feel good. She knew that Angel is Dereck's friend too but she did not like her getting involved in their problem. It was their family problem.

"It's okay. As you said, I'll just leave it to Him. And wait." Again, she finished her thoughts.

Stephen joined them all of a sudden. He was holding a box of chocolate for her. "Have a one, Claire."

"Awww, Stephen... How did you know I needed one?"

"Well...I know you enough to know?" Both of them laughed.

"You two seemed really close," Angelica commented.

"You could say that," Jamaica said.

"How did you two meet?" The nurse turned to Stephen.

He ate one chocolate before answering. "I was a fellow in a hospital in Canada. That's where she's going for her check-ups. We bumped into each other and I helped her to her doctor. That's it."

Jamaica added, "That's why when I needed to have an internship and my residency, he was the one who helped me get accepted."

"Wow, for seven years huh? I envy your friends because we just met again now."

"That's okay. We have a long time to catch up." She lightly nudged Angelica's shoulder.

Eating another chocolate, Stephen realized that he needed to step up his game. I have to formally court her now or I'll lose my chance. He glanced at Jamaica and smiled.

After their shift ended, he looked for Jamaica and saw her at the nurses' station. "Doc Jamaica, are you finished with your shift now?"

"I'm just checking a few things then I'll head out. Why?"

"I'll wait for you and send you home."

Hearing that, the nurses started teasing them.

"I'm good, I'll just take the bus."

"Doc Jam, don't be shy. Just accept Doc Stephen's offer." A nurse said.

Jamaica looked at him so he acted cutely. "Fine. Fine. You win."

She left the nurses' station to get her bag. Stephen winked at the nurse and said thanks.

They were already on the road when he asked her. "Do you want to grab dinner first?"

"I promised to eat dinner with Camila. She's probably waiting for me now."

"Okay. Then I need to take you home fast."

An hour later, Stephen stopped his car in front of Jamaica's house. However, there was another car parked blocking the gate. "Huh? Who could that be?" Jamaica mumbled to herself.

Both of them got out of the car and entered the house. "Mommy!" Camila ran to Jamaica and hugged her. "Hello, Daddy Stephen!"

"Hi, Princess." Stephen kneeled and Camila kissed him on the cheek.

"Mister played with me, Mommy. He said we'll go to the amusement park."

Stephen and Jamaica glanced at Dereck who was sitting comfortably on the couch. He smugly smiled and waved at them. "Hi!"

Chapter 10

Around the afternoon, Dereck visited Jamaica's ancestral house with the hope that they were staying there.

He got out of the car and saw their daughter playing in the front yard with her dolls.

Camila used a doll and said with a tiny voice, "Hey Camila, where is your daddy?"

Then she answered, "I don't know. Mommy told me he's busy but she'll introduce him one day. Maybe. When I ask Mommy she becomes sad so I said that I'm okay if I don't meet him. I don't like seeing Mommy cry."

The doll replied, "You're a good kid, Camila. Mommy loves you a lot."

"I love her too. More than she knows."

Dereck stepped back and hit his car making the alarm go off. He saw that Camila noticed him and made her way toward the gate. "Mister! You're the one we saw at the mall! Why are you here?"

Yaya Mel came out of the house in a hurry. "Camila? Who are you talking to?" She narrowed her eyes to see who it was. However, she still couldn't identify the man so she walked to the gate. "Dereck, dear, is that you?"

He was surprised to see the old woman. She was now older than before but still, she was beautiful. Dereck cleared his throat. "Hi, Yaya Mel. Long time no see."

The old lady smiled. "Come in, come in." She opened the gate for him.

"No, I'm fine. I just visited. I thought no one was staying here."

"Oh, don't be silly. Come inside and have an afternoon snack."

He felt embarrassed to decline the offer so he followed Yaya Mel inside the house.

Dereck glanced at Camila who was looking at him with so much curiosity. "Hi!" He waved at her.

Camila ignored him and ran inside.

Yaya Mel chuckled, "Sorry about that. She's like her mother. It takes a lot of time before you can get close to her."

He only smiled because he didn't know what to say. Entering the house, memories came flashing into his mind.

"Sit first," The old woman pointed at the couch in the living room. "I'll bring you snacks."

Dereck remembered the time when they would arrive there from school, he would have dinner with Jamaica and her parents. He was a family to them.

Realizing that, he felt awfully ashamed for the first time in his life. He took everything for granted. He never appreciated Jamaica's presence; only when she was already gone.

A tear escaped from the corner of his eye and Camila noticed it. "Why are you crying, Mister?" She pouted as her big black eyes stared widely at him.

He wiped away the tears and smiled. "It's nothing." Dereck paused. "I thought you're not talking to me?"

"Well..." The little girl glanced at her toys on the floor. "Do you want to play with me, Mister?"

"Sure. What are we playing?" He sat down on the carpet beside his daughter.

"Barbie!"

Dereck cracked up. She sure knows how to lose my cool.

"Dereck, have a break first," Yaya Mel was holding a tray with two slices of chocolate cake and two glasses of cold soda. "Darling, eat this first." Glancing at his wristwatch, he saw that it was just four in the afternoon. "Jamaica's shift ends at six in the evening so she usually arrives around seven-thirty. Are you okay waiting for her until that time?"

"Oh," he paused, "yes, I'm fine. I'll just play with Camila."

"So, you'll also join us for dinner? What would you like to have?"

"Your Chop Suey is still my favorite." He warmly smiled at the elder.

"It's my favorite too!" Camila joined their conversation. The corners of her mouth were filled with chocolate icing.

Yaya Mel and Dereck laughed at her face. "Wait, I'll get a tissue."

"Let me get it for you." He stood up and went to the kitchen. He still remembered where the things were kept. Dereck took the kitchen towel and pulled a ply. He came back to the living room and wiped the icing off his daughter's lips and cheeks. He stared at Camila's jet-black eyes that were so similar to his. All of a sudden, he felt a strong urge to embrace her.

Dereck engulfed her in his arms and tightened them around her small body. "M-mister, I-I can't breathe." He loosened his hold and apologized.

He cleared his throat. "Sorry." Dereck glanced at Yaya Mel and saw she was smiling while watching them.

"I better start preparing for dinner." She walked away leaving the two alone.

When he was about to eat his share of the cake, Camila was already taking a bite from it. "Hey!"

She giggled naughtily. "I thought you won't eat it, Mister. Mommy told me not to waste food." Camila was licking her fork then she burped loudly.

Turning to Dereck, she saw how bewildered he was then laughed loudly.

He shook his head and asked, "Is that you? How could you burp like a boy?"

"I did not!" Camila pouted. Her eyebrows knitted in annoyance. It was his time to tease her.

"Yes, you just did."

"No, I didn't!" Tears began streaming down her beautiful face. She wailed.

Dereck panicked. He had no idea how to stop her from crying. His face lit up when he remembered what to do. She was defenseless. Camila was not aware of what he was planning until he placed his fingers on her sides and tickled her.

Laughing, she began dancing just to get away from him. "Mister!" Camila ran away but he chased her. She squealed running around the living room until Dereck finally caught her.

"Gotcha!" He hugged her from the back and pulled her to sit. She was sitting on his lap as they pant trying to catch their breath.

He felt that he was a bit closer to Camila now. And he was happy with that. Dereck did not have any intention to have a paternity test from the start. He threw away the samples Jamaica gave him at the coffee shop.

What he was angry about was the fact that she did not tell him. It felt so unfair that he was not able to be part of their daughter's life when she was born. Because of that, he needs to catch up on all the lost time. "By the way, Princess, do you want to go to the amusement park?"

Camila nodded excitedly. "When are we going?"

"Let's ask you Mommy when she comes home."

"Okay!"

Hours later, Dereck and Camila heard the sound of a car engine. She began jumping up and down. "It's Mommy and Daddy Stephen!"

Dereck watched his daughter as she waited for her mother in front of the door. It opened wide and revealed Jamaica. "Mommy!" Camila hugged her. "Hello, Daddy Stephen!"

"Hi, Princess." Stephen kneeled and Camila kissed him on the cheek.

"Mister played with me, Mommy. He said we'll go to the amusement park." She was looking at her mother excited to hear her reply.

Stephen and Jamaica glanced at him. He smugly smiled and waved at them. "Hi!"

He saw Jamaica's mood change. "What are you doing here?" She pulled Camila towards her.

"Jamaica, Stephen, Dereck, it's time for dinner." Yaya Mel called them to the dining room. Everything was already set so they all sat down on the chairs and started eating.

Camila sat down beside her mother while Dereck and Stephen were sitting on the other side across from them and Yaya Mel was on one end.

"I prepared your favorites." There was a plate of Chop suey, a plate of Pineapple Chicken, and a plate of Bicol Express or Spicy Pork Stew.

"Yaya you didn't have to prepare so many dishes," Jamaica said.

"It's fine. I was glad to see Dereck again after a long time." The old lady smiled at him.

Dereck smiled back.

The atmosphere in the dining room never felt so awkward for Jamaica.

"Hey," Yaya Mel called the attention of Dereck and Stephen. "Stop staring at them.

Dereck cleared his throat while Stephen lowered his head and ate. Camila was the only one making noise and making everyone laugh at her silly antics.

After the meal, the guys bid goodbye. Jamaica blew out the air she had been holding in.

She and Camila went upstairs to rest for a while before washing up. They were on the bed sitting comfortably. "What did you and Mister talk about?" she asked her daughter.

"We didn't talk, Mommy. We only played." Camila answered. "Oh, he cried then he hugged me. Then we ate chocolate cake. Well, I ate his cake." She said with a giggle, recalling her mischievous deed.

Jamaica was staring into space. "Mommy, can we go to the amusement park with Mister?"

She bit her lip and thought about it. "We'll talk about it." Jamaica did not want to disappoint her daughter.

Stephen was driving home and his mind was still occupied by what happened earlier. Why did he have to be there? He'll ruin my plan." He wanted to drink his frustrations away so he looked for a bar.

Rowena's. It was the name of the restaurant and bar. H mmm... This place looks interesting, he thought. Stephen parked his car in front of the building and turned off the engine.

He got out and stepped inside the restaurant. It was an industrial bar and restaurant. From its wide windows to its hanging lamp, there was a homey vibe in it.

What made it more special was the band that was performing on the mini stage that he noticed the moment he entered.

The band was playing a jazz song and the voice of the singer was suited well. She was singing Can't Take My Eyes Off You.

And it literally did. Stephen couldn't take his eyes off the singer especially when he recognized that it was none other than Rosette! Her voice was so heavenly. It's melting his insides and his knees went weak.

Stephen held onto the counter for support. "Are you okay, Sir?" One of the staff asked.

"Yeah, I'm fine." He sat on the high chair by the bar counter. The bartender was busy mixing drinks for other customers. Stephen was about to order when he heard Rosette talk.

"Good evening, ladies and gentlemen, for tonight's show you can request songs by writing the title on a small note and passing it to our staff. I would also like to acknowledge our talented band, The One Quartet. For our next song, we'll perform Say You Love Me by MYMP.

He was enchanted by her. It felt like she was talking to him. That the song was for him. His heart began beating loudly so he placed a hand on his chest. Stephen used the heart rate checker in his fitness tracker watch. "116. I'm not even running."

"Can I have water?" He asked the bartender. After finishing the glass of water nothing happened so he ordered a few hard drinks. Hours later, he was already drunk.

"Sir, we're about to close now." The staff told him but he was not responding.

"What happened?"

"He's totally drunk. We need to send him home."

A woman tapped his shoulder. "Sir, sir, wake up. You need to go home. Where do you live?" Stephen turned to her.

"Rosette?" His voice was high and he kept blinking his eyes to see properly.

"Doc Stephen? What are you doing here?"

He fell asleep before he could answer.

The next day, Stephen woke up in an unfamiliar room. Huh? Where am I? The room was designed with beige walls and white furniture. He slowly sat up and hissed in pain when he felt his head breaking. Looking around, he saw posters of musicals, stuffed toys, and a working table.

He glanced at his side and noticed the picture frame on the bedside table. The picture was of a little girl around seven or eight years old and has very very long hair. This girl seems familiar.

"Doc, are you awake now?" The door opened, surprising him. Rosette was standing by the doorway with a grin on her face.

Chapter 11

Rosette sent the band to the door as they were cleaning the bar for closing. "We'll get going now, Rose. We still have work tomorrow."

"Thanks for playing tonight. I enjoyed it very much."

"You can apply as our main vocalist, you know," the guitarist jokes. The driver honked, getting his attention. "Anyway, see you some other time. Bye."

"Bye, take care." She waved and then closed the glass doors. Rosette noticed the man sleeping by the counter when she turned around. Rain, her cousin was waking him up. "What happened?"

"He's totally drunk. We need to send him home." Rain said.

Rosette tapped the man's shoulder. "Sir, sir, wake up. You need to go home. Where do you live?"

The man stirred and turned his face. He slowly blinked his eyes trying to recognize her. "Rosette?"

"Doc Stephen? What are you doing here?"

Stephen did not respond and slept instead.

She asked her cousin's help to take Stephen upstairs to her room. Rosette and Rain grunted while putting him to bed carefully. She placed a blanket over him. "Leave him to me."

"Are you sure?"

"Yeah, he's my doctor. I'll just leave him here and stay with Mom in her room."

"Okay. I'll finish cleaning downstairs then lock the doors." Rosette nodded. "Goodnight."

"Goodnight." Rain exited her room leaving them alone.

She stared at Stephen's sleeping face. Rosette caressed his face. "I hope someday I'll be the one in your eyes." She was about to leave him when he grabbed her wrist.

Glancing at her arm, Rosette then looked at Stephen. He was not saying anything so she removed his hand and left him.

The following day, she woke up earlier than usual. Her mother was already gone from the bed so Rosette immediately made her bed and headed downstairs. "Mom! Good morning!"

"Good morning." Rowena was in the kitchen frying some sunny-side-up eggs. "Dear, can you toast some bread and get avocados in the fridge to slice into thin pieces."

"Okay." She followed what her mother instructed. They were done preparing the food a minute later.

"Wake Doctor Stephen up. He'll be late for work." Rosette glanced at their wall clock. It was fifteen minutes before seven. She was about to go up the stairs when her phone rang.

"Hello?"

"Rosette, meet me at the dance studio later. I have something to discuss with you." Dereck asked.

"See you." She ended the call and went to her room. Rosette knocked on the door and slowly opened it. "Doc, are you awake now?" She peeked and then opened the door widely with a large grin. "Good morning, Doc, let's have breakfast."

Stephen looked at the picture he was holding and then at her. "Are you the little girl here in the photo?"

Rosette walked to the bed. "Yeah, that's me. Why?"

"Nothing. Have we met before? When you were 8 years old?"

She looked up rubbing her chin. "Hmmm... I don't remember." Rosette gazed back at him. "Anyway, wash up now then come down to eat. You'll be late for work."

He got out of bed easily because of his long legs and stood a foot taller than her. "Where's the bathroom?"

Going outside of the room, she guided him to the comfort room. "I'll go down now. The dining room is on the right side downstairs."

Stephen nodded so she left him there.

He was so sure she had met Rosette before. But where? He washed his face in the sink and looked at himself in the mirror. Stephen looked around the room and noticed how neat and organized it was.

He went downstairs and joined Rowena and Rosette for breakfast. "Doc, have a seat."

"Thank you." He looked at all the food on the table. "Wow! These all look delicious!" Besides the breakfast Rowena prepared, she also took out her best sellers in the restaurant like Honey Garlic Chicken, Asado, and Salad in Apple Cider Vinegar."Right? Mom cooked all of those. Some are the food we prepare at the restaurant." Rosette said.

Stephen smiled as he saw Rowena put garlic rice on his plate. "You should eat more while you're here, Doc. You're so skinny."

"Don't worry, Doc, you are not. Mom thinks all lean people are thin." Rosette explained with a laugh. Then Rowena did not put any rice on her daughter's plate. "Hey, Mom, where's mine?"

"You should diet. You're fat."

"I'm just chubby, Mom." She scrunched up her face making Stephen chuckle.

"Let's eat." Rowena said, "By the way, Doc, are you living with your family?"

"They are still in the States, Ma'am."

"Oh, don't need to call me Ma'am. Just call me Auntie."

"Okay, Auntie. Please call me by my first name, Stephen." He smiled at the old woman then shifted his gaze at Rosette who was already filling her mouth with food. She looks cute.

His eyebrows knitted. What am I saying? Stephen shook his head to erase the thought.

"You don't like the food?" Rowena asked with a concerned look in her eyes.

"No, it's not that. It's very delicious. I like it." He cleared his throat and focused on eating. He casually glanced at Rosette then their eyes met. Stephen choked on his food.

Rosette hurriedly poured water into an empty glass and handed it to him. "Are you okay?"

He nodded, coughing.

Rowena glanced at the wall clock. "You're going to be late to the hospital.

"It's my day off today."

"Really?" Rosette exclaimed. "What do you do on your day off?"

"Most of the time I stay at home and sleep."

The three of them talked about random things during the meal.

"Thanks for the meal." Stephen was about to leave.

"You're welcome. You can come anytime you want." Rowena told him.

"I'll leave now." He lowered his head a little.

"Wait! Doc!" Rosette ran outside wearing a carrot-colored above-the-knee dress and white sneakers. "Can you drop me off at the dance studio?"

He frowned. "What are you going to do there?"

"Direk has something to discuss with me. Why?"

"Nothing." He tried to calm down and remove the frown on his face. "Let's go."

"Take care, you two."

Inside the car, Stephen was in deep thought. Stephen, why are you getting annoyed? That's Rosette! She is not Jamaica. Why do you care so much?

"Doc?" Rosette glanced at him. "Doc," she called again, "what are you thinking?"

"Huh?"

"You're too quiet."

"Oh," he only smiled. Their quick trip felt like a long one.

Rosette got out of the car. "Thanks for the ride, Doc." She closed the door.

He left after seeing her get inside the building. Going on his way home, Stephen finally remembered who she was. "It's her! The ponytail girl! She didn't even remember me."

Ten years ago, he worked as an orderly in a provincial hospital as part of his internship. He was assigned to the Pediatrics Department, and one patient was always trying to escape from the hospital.

The little girl disliked being hospitalized because injections were painful and doctors were scary. He befriended her and eventually, the girl got close to him. That's why she didn't want to leave when she was discharged. She cried her eyes out so he made a promise to her.

"We'll see each other again when you grow up."

"When is that?" Her wide eyes stared at him.

"Someday."

"Promise?"

"Promise." They made a pinky swear and he watched the kid leave the hospital. She was waving at him with a huge smile on her face.

Dereck was typing the edited script on his laptop. It was the script he wrote three years ago entitled It Takes Two to Tango. It was the story of him and Jamaica and their confusing relationship of push and pull. But now, there was a change in the storyline. When Camila joined the picture.

He stopped typing and mumbled to himself, "What can be the best ending for this one?"

Rosette barged into his office. "Hi, Direk? What are you doing? Why did you call me?"

"I want you to read this script." He stood up with the laptop in his hand. Dereck gave it to her when she sat on the couch.

"Ooohhh... Nice title, It Takes Two to Tango. What genre is this?"

"I don't know. You tell me."

She read the script and asked. "Is this your story? And Jamaica?"

"It's about the two of us. But it's not a love story, okay?" He denied.

"Oh, come on! It's so obvious!"

A few minutes later, Rosette gave the laptop back to him. "So, how will the story end?"

"I'm still thinking about it."

"Oh," she had an idea. "Maybe you can use that for your proposal."

"Proposal to what?"

"You know when you ask Jamaica to get married."

Dereck laughed. "I'm not even courting her. How can I marry her?"

"Why? You won't do anything? I thought you wanted a complete family. And that's what I can tell from the script you made."

"I-I..." I don't know what I feel about her.

Rosette sighed. "You know what, nothing will happen if you won't take the first step. Do you think Jamaica will wait for you forever? Is Jamaica even waiting for you now? Letting you meet your daughter doesn't mean she wants to have a relationship with you."

"Isn't it supposed to be like that? Since we have Camila?"

"No. You still have to win Jamaica's heart, Direk." She glanced at the wall clock inside the office. "Time is ticking. Every second counts. And the longer you delay your plans the farther she's getting away.

"By the way, what about the paternity test you were asking? What's your plan about that?"

"You don't need to look for one anymore."

"Do you believe now that she's your daughter?"

"No." But I feel it. And if she's the only connection I have with Jamaica. I'll try to do everything I can.

He was alarmed. All this time he felt relaxed that everything would go according to his plan when he remembered Stephen, his competition.

Dereck never thought he would have a rival in winning Jamaica's love and affection. He believed she would never have a change of heart. The Jamaica he knew was someone who would give everything to him and he was confident to a hundred percent she was still like that.

All of a sudden, he recalled how awkward Jamaica acted when he visited them. He could tell in her face that she wanted him out of that house. And out of her life.

"What should I do now?" Dereck asked Rosette.

She grinned. "You really can't do anything without me, huh? If I'll help you, will you give me the lead role for this play?"

"Let's see about that. Of course, you have to audition first."

"Direk!"

Jamaica was already preparing Camila for bed when her phone rang. Dereck was making a video call. Before answering, she stood in front of the mirror and checked herself. She brushed her hair using her hands. "Hello?"

He made an awkward wave. "Hi!" Then he scratched the back of his head.

"Why did you suddenly call?" Jamaica tucked her hair behind her ear.

Camila noticed it was a video call so she joined in the conversation. "Hey, Mister!" She waved at him with a smile while on all fours on the bed.

"Princess!" His smile almost reached from ear to ear. "I called to ask if you want to go to the Amusement park on Sunday."

"Really?" Camila turned to her mother asking, "Mommy, can we go?"

"I think there's no problem with that. What time should we meet at the amusement park?"

"I'll pick you up at nine in the morning," Dereck told Jamaica then talked to their daughter again. "You should sleep now, Princess, or else you'll have black eyes like your Mommy."

Camila looked at Jamaica closely. "That's because Mommy is working very hard. I won't have that because I only sleep and play."

Jamaica chuckled at the kid's response. She's like an adult when she talks.

"Well, I can't argue with that!" Dereck smiled and she felt he was looking directly at her eyes. Wait, hold on! What is he doing? Is he flirting?

"Mister, do you like my Mommy?"

Chapter 12

"**M**ister, do you like my Mommy?" Camila asked him. And he did not expect that so he laughed it off.

"Why did you ask, Princess?"

"I think you like her." But I'm never even showing it! He thought.

"Camila, stop saying nonsense."

"But Mommy-"

"Go to sleep now." Jamaica looked at the phone again. "See you on Sunday."

"O-okay. Bye." Jamaica ended the call.

Dereck lay down on the bed and stared at the ceiling. He closed his eyes and imagined the three of them having a great time together. That scene in his mind drew a smile on his face and made his heart thump loudly. He was somewhat excited about their family date.

"Wait," he sat back up, "I'm not excited to see her. I'm going there to have a bonding experience with my daughter."

The day he had been waiting for had finally come. Even before the sun broke out, Dereck was already outside and had run around the park. He reached their apartment and saw that Rosette was already there. "Good morning, Direk!"

"Why are you so early?" He was wiping his cheek with his towel.

"Of course! I'm punctual!" She turned to Adrian who was lying down on the couch. "Hey, Adrian, let's go to the amusement park."

"I don't want to." He answered lethargically. She stood by the couch and pulled his arm.

"No, you need to come."

"I don't want to." He was so strong that she let him go.

"Let him be." Dereck drank water. "You actually don't need to come."

"But I want to watch you three." He glared at her but she just mischievously smiled. "Fine, fine. I'll go home now."

"Bye, just lock the door." Dereck went to the bathroom for a shower.

He stood in front of his full-length mirror an hour later, Dereck was dressed in a light blue shirt and denim jeans. He styled his hair before going out of the room.

"Adrian, don't forget to eat." After putting on his black basketball shoes, he left their house.

Dereck arrived at Jamaica's place at exactly nine a.m. He pulled out his phone from his pocket and called her. "I'm here outside."

"Okay, we'll go out now."

He then heard the front door open. Jamaica and Camila were stepping out of the house. Jamaica was looking gorgeous in her maroon puff short-sleeve ruffle collar below-the-knee dress and white sneakers.

Their daughter ran to the gate wearing her denim jumpers and cute white shoes. Her long black hair was waving along with her every movement. She waited for her mother to unlock it. Dereck saw Camila waving at him with a huge grin. His car was tinted so she couldn't see him so he opened his window and waved back at her.

"Mister!" She jumped up and down.

Jamaica unlocked the gate. Dereck got off the driver's seat and opened the backseat for Camila. "Princess, get in."

After locking the gate again, Jamaica turned to the passenger's seat to also get in. She was surprised to see Dereck open the door for her. "T-thanks."

He closed the door and ran to the driver's seat to get in. Buckling his seatbelt, Dereck started the engine and then glanced at the rearview mirror. "Princess, are you ready?"

"Yes, Mister!" She giggled excitedly.

Jamaica was just looking outside while Camila was singing in a very low voice. This is so awkward, he thought. "I'll play some music. Princess, do you have any songs you like?"

"Yes. Do you have songs by IU, Mister?"

"IU? Who is that?"

"A Korean singer! You should listen to her songs. It's so beautiful, right Mommy?" Jamaica just nodded. She was starting to get sleepy.

"Okay. Can you look for songs here on my phone?" Camila took it and searched the music app then the song started playing inside the car.

"Here's your phone, Mister."

"Thanks, Princess." He took back his phone and put it in his pocket. "By the way," Dereck glanced at the rearview mirror again, "Can you stop calling me 'Mister'? Why do you keep calling me that?"

"Because I don't know your name?" She looked back at him through the mirror and saw his amused expression. Camila wiggled her eyebrows which earned a hearty laugh from him.

"Call me Daddy Dereck, okay?"

"I don't want to. It's long."

"But you call Stephen 'Daddy'."

"That's because he took care of me when I was a baby. And I'm planning to marry him someday."

Oh no, you won't. His eyebrows knitted in annoyance. He then peeked in Jamaica's direction and saw she was sleeping.

"Mommy only has a few hours of sleep every day. After putting me to sleep she goes to her study room and reads books all night. Still, she makes time for me and takes care of me."

Dereck noticed Jamaica was getting cold so he asked their daughter to hand the jacket beside her. He put it on her when they reached a stoplight.

Camila was just watching how her father placed the jacket on her mother. She smiled at his sweetness. But that was not enough proof that he really cares for them.

Three and a half hours later, they were already in the amusement park's parking lot. "We're here!" Dereck announced.

Jamaica slowly opened her eyes and yawned tiredly. She covered her mouth with both hands and then stretched her arms upward. She forgot he was there watching her.

Turning immediately to Dereck, Jamaica saw he was leaning on the chair with his arms crossed over his chest.

"Good afternoon, Mommy?"

"Huh?"

"Are you ready now? Let's find a restaurant to eat at." Dereck got out of the car and then opened the backseat to carry Camila in his arms.

Jamaica followed them to the amusement park's entrance. "Wait," the two looked back at her. "Sweetheart, I'll tie your hair first." Dereck put Camila down so she ponytailed their daughter's hair. "There. All done."

"Let's go." He carried Camila again. "Where do you want to eat?" Dereck asked her.

Camila pointed at a fast-food restaurant. "I want chicken and spaghetti there."

"Do you really want to eat there?" Jamaica noticed a sudden change in Dereck's face. He turned pale. She tilted her head in curiosity.

"Yes!"

He cleared his throat and then said, "Okay." Dereck looked at her calling her attention so she ran to his side and they stepped inside the restaurant.

Rosette was at home when she called her doctor. "Hello, Doc Stephen?"

"Yes, Ms. Morales? Do you have any problems?"

"Why are you calling me 'Ms. Morales'? Call me by my first name."

Stephen laughed. "Fine. So, why did you call, Rosette?"

"Are you free right now?"

"Would I be answering your phone if I'm not free?"

She rolled her eyes at him even though he couldn't see her. "Anyway, do you want to go to the amusement park today?"

"Hmm... I don't think my body's ready for taking rides today. This old man is dead tired from working 'til three in the morning."

"It means you can't come with me, right?" Her voice instantly changed.

"Oh, alright, I'll go with you. I'll pick you up at your house in an hour."

"Yehey! You're not spoiling me, aren't you?"

"No, you're spoiling yourself." Stephen retorted with a chuckle. "I'll hang up now so I can get ready."

"Okay, see you later." She had a cunning grin on her beautiful face. "Oh!" Rosette remembered to look for something good to wear. She settled in a white crop top shirt and denim wide-leg trousers matching it with gray high sole sneakers. She braided her hair and put on a little makeup.

"Rose! Stephen is outside!" Rowena yelled at her daughter from downstairs.

"He's here already?" Rosette panicked. She hasn't finished getting ready yet. An hour flew by fast! "Wait! I'm coming down now!" She ran downstairs straight outside and saw Stephen was leaning on the car waiting for her. "Doc!"

"Ready?"

"Yeah!"

"Hey lady, care to tell me where you're going?" Her mother asked.

"Sorry Auntie, I invited Rosette to have fun at the amusement park."

"Really? Okay. Be careful and enjoy, kids."

The two got inside the car and went on the road.

Camila had been riding the carousel seven times in a row. "Sweetheart, don't you want to try other rides?"

"No, I've always wanted to go here."

"We come here most of the time," Jamaica said.

"Yeah, but-" this is the first time we're here with Daddy, she finished in her thoughts while gazing at Dereck.

He stared back at her and smiled. "Are you happy right now?"

The little girl nodded. He patted her head. "Just let me know if you want to come here again, okay?" Camila smiled. Deep inside she wanted that to happen. She already knew Dereck even before they accidentally met at the mall.

One time she was reading books from her mother's bookshelves when a photo album caught her eye. There was nothing written on it and there were no photos.

Camila was about to put it back when something fell.

It was the only picture in there. A photo of her parents. Dereck had his arm around Jamaica's shoulder and they were smiling from ear to ear. On the back of it, there was a single word written on it. 'Camila'. That was how she discovered who her Daddy was.

The carousel ride ended so Jamaica suggested they try another ride. The three of them looked for a bench to sit on first and relax.

"Princess, do you like that?" Dereck pointed his finger at the cotton candy stand just around the corner. Camila nodded so he ran to the seller and bought three. Walking his way back to the bench, he saw how Jamaica took care of their daughter. She was placing a towel on her back and putting a lot of powder. He noticed how weary Jamaica looked and it made him want to take care of her.

Smiling, he ran to them and handed them the cotton candies. "Here you go." Dereck sat down beside Camila. "Where are we going next?"

"Do you want to try the Ferris Wheel?" Jamaica suggested. "I want to see the whole place."

"Let's go." Automatically, Dereck took his daughter's hand and they walked together. Jamaica ran after them.

"Why are you leaving me?"

He chuckled heartily. "It's because you have short legs. Right, Princess?"

Camila looked up at him and smiled back. She stopped walking and raised her arms, asking Dereck to carry her.

He bent a little and pulled her into his arms. "Are you tired?"

"No, I just want Mister to carry me." She tightly circled her arms around his neck.

Jamaica noticed it and looked at Dereck with a curious stare. Her eyes met his. Both of them had the same expression on their faces.

"Direk!" Someone called Dereck so he and Jamaica turned in the voice's direction. It was Rosette waving at them with two hands.

Squinting his eyes, Dereck asked. "Who is she with?"

"Isn't that Stephen?"

"Stephen?"

Jamaica nodded. "Yes, Stephen, my colleague."

He rolled his eyes though she did not see him. Colleague, my foot, he thought.

Camila heard Stephen's name so she looked around for him. "Where's Daddy Stephen?" She tried getting down from Dereck's hold and then ran towards the doctor. "Daddy Stephen!"

Jamaica ran after her and so did Dereck.

"Daddy Stephen!" The little girl embraced her favorite person next to her mom.

"Hello, Princess, how are you?"

"I'm good. Are you also riding the Ferris wheel?"

"Yes. You too?"

"Uh-huh," Camila looked at Rosette and asked. "Who is she? Is she your girlfriend, Daddy?"

"Yes! I am his girlfriend." She crossed her arms over her chest and lowered her head to meet Camila in the eyes.

Stephen held Rosette at her arm to stop her from saying nonsense.

Camila suddenly sobbed, getting the attention of other people in the amusement park. Jamaica and Dereck walked to her and crouched down. "Sweetheart, stop crying."

"Princess, do you want ice cream?" Dereck tried to console their daughter.

Frowning, Camila said to Rosette. "Daddy Stephen likes me more!"

Chapter 13

Stephen and Rosette arrived at the amusement park. She excitedly got out of the car and exclaimed, "Wow! The last time I went here was when I was seven years old."

"Really?" Stephen closed the door and locked his car.

"Yup," she paused, "What about you, Doc?" Rosette turned to him.

"I've never been to one before." He stood beside her, appreciating the beauty of the place.

The amusement park had a huge entrance where people were coming in. What stood out the most was the huge Ferris wheel.

"Does this mean this is your first time?"

"Yeah."

"Well, then, let's go." She grabbed his hand and pulled him with her. They went to the ticket booth to buy two tickets. Rosette was pulling out some cash from her pocket when Stephen stopped her.

"Let me pay for it."

"No, you don't have to. Just pay for all our food once we're in."

"Okay." They stood in line at the entrance. "So, what do you want to do? Do you want to enjoy the rides or eat first?"

"It's better to try the rides first," Stephen said then pulled her to the kart game.

The two of them enjoyed each other's company. He was able to forget Jamaica but it was just for a short while. The next thing he knew, she was standing in front of him with Camila and Dereck.

Camila ran up to him and hugged him tightly.

"Hello, Princess, how are you?" he asked, avoiding looking Jamaica in the eyes.

"I'm good. Are you also riding the Ferris wheel?"

"Yes. You too?"

"Uh-huh," Camila noticed the lady she was with and asked, "Who is she? Is she your girlfriend, Daddy?" Her eyes were starting to get watery.

"Yes! I am his girlfriend." Rosette crossed her arms over her chest, bent her body, and stared at the little girl teasingly.

"Stop making fun of her," Stephen whispered in her ear. Rosette bit her lower lip to stop herself from laughing.

Camila suddenly sobbed, surprising all of them. Worried, Jamaica and Dereck approached their daughter. They crouched down and consoled her. "Sweetheart, stop crying."

"Princess, do you want ice cream?" Dereck tried to console their daughter.

Frowning, Camila said to Rosette. "Daddy Stephen likes me more!"

Stephen would have been ecstatic hearing that if only it was like before. However, seeing the complete family they are; realizing he was never in the picture, to begin with, he needed to settle his feelings for Jamaica. Quietly and as normally as he could.

For the first time, his heart and his mind did not go in sync. He wanted to handle the situation as calmly as possible but his feelings told him otherwise. So he took Rosette's hand and clasped it to his cold one then left the three without saying anything.

"Doc," Rosette called, "Doc!" Still, he was dragging her outside the park. "Stephen!"

He stopped in his tracks and glanced at her. There he realized what he had just done.

"Can you let go of my hand now?" Rosette was frowning and removed her hand from his grasp. "Why did you suddenly grab my hand and leave? I was just joking and I didn't mean to make her cry."

Stephen felt guilty. They weren't even inside for an hour yet. "Sorry," he sighed. "Do you want to go in again? I'll buy the tickets."

"No, let's just eat and then go home." She headed to the parking lot and looked for his car.

Stephen sighed again and ran after her.

Dereck and Jamaica brought their daughter to an ice cream parlor to stop her from crying. It was very effective! They only bought her a huge bowl of banana splits filled with chocolate syrup.

"Sweetheart, do you want to go home after finishing that?"

Camila nodded while she was still busy with her ice cream. Dereck was sitting beside her wiping the corner of her mouth and her cheeks. He turned to Jamaica, "Aren't you hungry?"

"I'm fine. Maybe I'll just cook at home." Suddenly her stomach growled loud enough for him to hear.

Dereck stifled a laugh and it made her embarrassed more. "I think we need to eat now. Wait here, I'll order from the other store. What do you want?

"I don't know. I'll just have what you want to eat."

A few minutes later, he came back carrying a paper bag. "What's that?"

He sat first before taking out what he ordered. "I saw your favorite Ebi burger and a lemonade."

"Y-you knew my favorite?" What Dereck said next surprised her even more.

"Of course. How couldn't I? I've been observing you."

"Y-you what?"

Dereck realized later what he had been confessing. "Oh," he avoided her stares. "It's nothing. Eat now."

"Where is yours?"

"I didn't buy one. I got full from all the snacks we've been eating."

Jamaica felt uncomfortable that he was not eating so she cut the burger in half. "Here, let's share." She also slid her lemonade closer to him. He gladly accepted her offer and sipped from the straw.

It was an unexpected gesture from her. He had never seen her act boldly like that when they were together. Dereck was surprised but he kept it to himself.

Once again he was silently watching her. The way she eats, drinks, and how she scrunches her nose and scratches it after. Jamaica then took the lemonade. "Wait-"

She looked at him after drinking from the same straw. "What?"

"I just drank from the straw."

"Oh, it slipped my mind."

It wasn't a big deal for him. What amused him was that it was not a big deal for 'her'.

She removed the straw and asked, "Are we good now?"

"That's not what I mean." Dereck finished his burger in two bites. He was just staring at Jamaica and he completely forgot their daughter beside him. He thought it was just the two of them having a date.

Camila burped loudly. "Camila! What did I say about doing that?"

Their little girl giggled. Dereck was enjoying himself watching the mother and daughter interact.

Jamaica shook her head and finished her burger instead.

Adrian was locked in his bedroom with a phone in his hand. He was stalking Angelica in her social media account if she had recent posts or any activities.

He read one of her posts.

I hope today was like yesterdays when you were beside me.

Many reacted to her post and most flooded her with comments asking who she was referring to but Angelica didn't leave any responses to any of those and it was making him curious. He had a hunch that it might be him she was talking about yet he'd rather not expect it.

Those are more hurtful than disappointments.

He sat up contemplating if he should send her a message or not. Adrian kept biting his lower lip. "Her father told me not to chat with her nor talk to her. I don't want to break my promise to him."

He remembered the time he met Mr. Alexander Garcia a month ago. The latter is their law firm because he was the former employer of Adrian's boss, Jason.

"Good morning, Mr. Garcia." Jason welcomed Alexander into his office.

What is he doing here? Adrian thought. He was flabbergasted to see him there.

Alexander sat on the couch as Jason prepared coffee for the two of them. "So, to what do I owe your sudden visit, Sir Alex?"

Adrian was fixing some documents on his boss' table as he listened to their conversation.

"I wanted to visit you and talk to someone." Mr. Garcia turned to him and gave him a meaningful look.

"Really?"

"Can you give me and Mr. Fernando here a minute?"

Jason was surprised and stopped what he was doing. "Oh," he paused, "Oh, sorry. I'll go out now."

When Adrian and Alexander were left alone in the office, Mr. Garcia told him to sit down.

"Why do you want to talk to me, Sir?"

"I discovered that you're the guy my daughter is dating. I also discovered that you don't have parents and you grew up in an orphanage."

"Yes, Sir, that's correct." He answered but he couldn't meet him in the eye. He felt ashamed of himself and he began having doubts.

"I don't want to intrude in my daughter's relationship. I just want the best for her."

"And you think I'm not 'the best' for her? I know I don't deserve your daughter but my feelings for her are sincere."

"You don't have to tell me. Just prove it." With that, Mr. Garcia left him alone in the room.

Jason came in running and asked him, "What did he say? Did he invite you to work in his firm?"

Adrian sighed and since then the remaining confidence he had to be in a relationship with Angelica vanished.

He plopped down on the bed and covered his face with a pillow then screamed at the top of his lungs. Remembering what happened only discourages him from pursuing Angelica; even clearing the misunderstanding between them.

Dereck was driving his way to take Jamaica and Camila home. Their daughter was sound asleep in the backseat hugging the stuffed toy he won at the dart game. "Why didn't you tell me about her?"

"Huh?" Jamaica was totally caught off guard by his question.

"If you were pregnant with her when you left. Why didn't you tell me about it? Didn't you trust me?" He did not notice his voice raise a little.

She played with her fingers fighting the nervousness she was feeling. It might be uncomfortable to talk about it on the road and eventually, it would be discussed, and now is the best time for that.

"I-I got scared."

"Scared of what?" Dereck peeked at her.

"That you will not take responsibility."

"Is that how you think of me?" he asked in a controlled voice. Camila suddenly moved from her sleep. "I wanted to talk to you after that night but you avoided me like I had some kind of disease."

"Because it was just a one-night stand." She was lowering her head and he couldn't understand what he was saying.

"What?"

"What happened to us was just a one-night stand!" Jamaica repeated it loud and clear. "We weren't even a couple. You didn't even like me." She looked at him, mad. Her eyes were speaking. Finally saying what she truly felt.

Dereck pulled over.

"What happened that night was just because you're drunk."

"But I remember everything."

"Were you ready that time? To have me and Camila at that time?"

He was speechless. "What?" he asked in a calmer voice. Dereck could see the pain in her eyes but he couldn't do anything.

And his reaction only proved one thing to her. Even now, he's not ready. Jamaica turned to face the window. "Just take us home. I don't actually expect anything from you. Knowing her existence was unexpected."

Dereck started the engine again and continued his drive. "Would I ever get to meet her if we didn't see each other at the mall?" He quietly asked, his eyes were on the road.

"Yeah. I was ready to go to you and tell you everything. Accept her or not I would still tell you."

He didn't say a word until he sent them home.

"Thanks for having time for her. I'll just find the right time to tell her that you're her dad."

He wanted to argue again but he held himself back. Jamaica got out of the car and opened the backseat to get Camila. She put on the backpack filled with Camila's things and then carried her and the stuffed toy. As soon as she closed the door, Dereck gassed up and left them standing in front of the house.

He was offended by all of the things he heard from Jamaica. She never said those kinds of words to him before. All she did was smile and just be there by his side. Be understanding and appreciative. All the time.

"Dereck, I think you just messed up big time." He mumbled to himself.

Chapter 14

After their 'argument', Dereck decided to stay away from Jamaica and Camila for almost half a month. He made up his mind not to go near them for a while until he settles his feelings.

While doing that, he started planning the play he wrote. He decided to create Tango as a one-time musical play and he had been planning everything for two weeks. He scouted Rosette as the main lead of the play. He also had auditions for the other roles and hired a technical team for the project.

"Are you really going to invest all your money in this project?" Rosette asked beside him.

"Yeah. Why?" Dereck's attention was still focused on the actors performing on stage.

"Are you really gonna do it?"

"Yes. Why do you keep asking me? Long before, I had already composed the songs too. I'm asking for help from a music producer I know."

"Wow! You're really motivated to do this, huh?"

"I think this is the only way to make it up to them."

"What do you mean?"

"Nothing." Dereck smiled and then yelled to everyone, "Let's take a break! Be back by one p.m."

The actors and staff dispersed one by one. Some went out to eat and some stayed to eat their packed lunch.

"Treat me to lunch, Direk." She said, "Let's have something fresh."

"Sure." They stood up from their seats and headed outside.

Dereck and Rosette felt the scorching heat piercing them like needles. Both of them were walking by the sidewalk to grab a meal in a nearby eatery. "Hey, do I look alright?" he stopped in his tracks facing the mirrored wall of a boutique to look at himself. Standing a hundred and eighty-seven tall, Dereck checked his face in the mirror. His right hand was on his unshaven chin, then scratched the top of his head.

Rosette rolled her eyes as she drank water from her jug. "As usual, you look like you haven't taken a bath for days, and seeing your dark circles, it looked like you stayed awake all night." She commented, stifling a laugh. The truth was, he's cute, but sadly not her type. There was someone else she liked. Someone she doesn't know.

"I stayed up all night. Do I look that bad?" He defended himself, trying to straighten his wrinkled shirt, and also sniffed his underarms.

She leaned closer and tried to sniff him when she immediately covered her nose with her fingers. "You stink! You badly need a shower!" Dereck narrowed his eyes at her, pouting.

They walked again as he removed the sand from his eyes. "Stop being conscious. It's your fault for not taking a bath and fixing yourself. You look like a mess." She shamelessly blurted on their way to the restaurant. It was only two blocks away from the theater.

He closed his eyes and exhaled deeply, controlling his temper. His hands balled into fists as he gritted his teeth. Dereck appreciated her frankness because it also helped him, especially in their musical plays, but most of the time, it annoyed the hell out of him because he wanted to smack her on the head.

Dereck opened the door to the eatery and heard the soothing white noise of the wind chimes. The place had a homey ambiance and home-cooked meals that made them come to eat there almost every day. Customers become regulars of the restaurant. The music also gave a different feel to the place.

Looking around, they searched for the best place to sit. Rosette instantly sat on the vacant seat at the farthest corner near the comfort room. "Direk, here! Hurry!" She called him, gesturing her hand for him to come over.

Both of them occupied the table as he shouted their orders. "We'll have the regular!"

"Hey! I want to order another meal!"

"You said it's my treat?" He reminded her. "That's the only thing I can afford now."

"What a stingy person."

While waiting, Dereck asked her, "Did you think about my offer?" He was tapping her fingers on the table as he laid back in his chair.

"Are you sure you want to sponsor me in college?" Rosette leaned on the table, crossing her arms.

"Yes. And in return, you just have to help me in managing the dance school and this theater group."

"I'll think about it."

"There's nothing to think about." Both of them laughed.

Their orders came and they hurriedly gobbled the meal down to go back again to the theater.

Among all the people on the rooftop, Stephen, Jamaica, and Angelica were the only quiet ones staring at their phones. They barely touched their food and it was already the end of their lunch break. Stephen couldn't decide if he would call or send a message to Rosette. He still felt embarrassed about his actions the other day at the amusement park.

Jamaica was staring at her phone waiting for Dereck's call every single day for two weeks. She was looking at her new wallpaper. It was their first family picture. After her outburst last time she wanted to take back everything she said. But she doesn't want to call him anymore. She wanted him to take the first step. She was determined for that to happen.

As for Angelica, she had been browsing Adrian's social media account and was looking for any signs that he had a new girlfriend already. However, his posts were only about random stuff. Now she's about to lose her mind trying to figure out what goes in his mind.

Stephen stood up from the bench and tried to peek at what the two were looking at but they instantly hid it.

"Our break's done. Let's go back to work." He said so Jamaica and Angelica followed him.

Stephen had a determined look on his face. He won't call or text her instead he will visit their restaurant again. Because it was Friday, the restaurant had an open concert.

Stephen hurriedly clocked out as soon as his shift ended. "Just call me when there's an emergency!" He shouted, instructing the nurses and residents. He ran to his car, started the engine, and made his way to their store.

He was in a hurry coming inside the restaurant. The moment he turned the knob and opened the door, Stephen instantly heard her sweet innocent voice filling his ears. She was singing her version of Crazy For You by Madonna. The band was playing its jazz version with a pianist, drummer, double bass player, and trumpet.

Rosette was smiling at the audience as she sang. Then their eyes met. She avoided his gaze and focused on finishing the song. He felt sad. Seeing her reaction was unexpected for him. Stephen sat on a high chair by the counter and watched her perform.

"Thank you," she said when the audience clapped. "Thank you for joining us tonight. I hope you're having a good time. For this next song, I need a partner. Does anyone want to have a duet with me?"

Stephen mustered his courage and walked up to the mini-stage. He saw the surprised expression on Rosette's face and it made him smile sheepishly. He bit his lower lip as she was still glancing at her.

Rosette handed her a microphone and then signaled the band to play the next song. She tiptoed and whispered in his ear. "Just look at the monitor for the lyrics."

He nodded, smiling. Looks like she's not mad anymore, Stephen thought. She smiled back then started singing. The song was Perfect Combination by Johnny Gill and Stacy Lattisaw.

Singing the song with her, it felt like every word was speaking to him.

Her eyes smiled when they looked at each other, making his heart flutter and filling his stomach with butterflies. He was melting with her every stare that his voice started to tremble still Rosette helped him finish the song.

"Ladies and gentlemen, let's give him a round of applause."

Stephen went back to his seat and waited for Rosette.

The jamming session ended after two hours of fun and laughter. Rosette was able to give a memorable night to those who visited their restaurant and that's enough for her. Although she was shocked to see Stephen plus the fact he sang with her. I'm on cloud nine, she thought.

Pretending she was still upset, Rosette approached him. "What are you doing here?"

"Uh, eating?"

She crossed her arms over her chest and rolled her eyes at him. "I can see that, Mister. I mean why are you here?"

Stephen cleared his throat and stood up. Rosette followed his movements with her gaze then looked up at him. "I wanted to apologize again for how I acted last time. I don't feel comfortable that I made you upset because you didn't get to enjoy the rides in the amusement park."

"Did you really think that was the reason why I was upset?"

He frowned, giving it a thought. "It isn't?"

Rosette snickered. "Anyway, I'm not mad so you didn't really have to come here."

"Are we good now?" Stephen asked. His face instantly lit up. He smiled like a little boy.

She squinted her eyes and had a deep thought. I feel like I've seen him before. "Have we met before, Doc?"

It was his turn to smirk. "Yes." He stifled a laugh. "I'll give you a reward if you remember who I am. I'll give you three tries to figure it out." Stephen turned his back on her. I'll go home now. See you."

Rosette was left there standing speechless. That was what she hated the most, guessing.

She was already in bed yet she couldn't sleep. Her mind was still occupied by what Stephen told her and kept on turning around the bed. "Where did I meet him?"

Stephen arrived home and took a quick shower. He was drying his hair when he remembered their duet earlier. He smiled at the thought.

Looking at the mirror, Stephen told himself. "Why are you smiling, huh?" he lightly hit his reflection in the mirror and hung his towel on a chair before jumping on the bed. His mind these past few days were filled with Rosette and her only.

He kept on removing Jamaica from his mind whenever she appears out of nowhere. He already knew Dereck won and there was no use fighting in a battle he wouldn't win. He was no risk-taker. And he could see in Jamaica's eyes that their story never ended. It didn't have the closure they really needed. It was still an open book that the writer decided to continue writing.

Stephen turned and reached the drawer of his bedside table. He opened it and picked a scrunchie. It was the scrunchie Rosette always used when she was staying in the hospital.

It was the summertime of 2012, and Stephen was taking a break in the hospital's playground. He was watching children play on the slides and swing. One kid caught his attention.

She had very long black hair. Because she was busy running around, it was disheveled and covered her cute little face. He had a rubber band so Stephen went up to her and tied her hair.

Rosette looked at him with a curious look. "Huh?" She touched her hair. "You tied my hair, Mister?" She stood up and smiled at him. "Thank you."

"You're welcome. What's your name?"

"Rose."

"Hi, Rose. Why are you here in the hospital?"

"My mom said it's because I'm tired in school." Stephen wanted to pinch her reddish cheeks."How long have you been here?"

"I don't know. Why are you here, Mister? Are you a doctor?"

"Not yet. But I will be. Someday." She nodded even though it was visible on her face that she did not understand a thing he said. He chuckled and patted her head. "Continue what you were doing. I'll go now. Bye!"

"Bye, Mister!" Rosette cutely waved at him with a huge smile on her face.

Chapter 15

Angelica was staring at the ceiling on her day off while lying in bed. She terribly misses Adrian.

She lay on her stomach and grabbed her phone from the bedside table. Opening the social media application, she checked Adrian's account if he had new posts or any updates.

Sadly, it was still the same. "Does this guy really like me?" Angelica turned again. "Why isn't he doing anything?"

She finally sat up and said, "Should I test him?" Dialing someone's number, she placed her phone on her left ear. "Hello?"

"Hey, Angel, what's up?"

"Hey Henry, can I ask you a favor?"

"What is it?"

"Can we go on a date?"

For a moment, Henry was not saying anything.

"Hello, Henry? Are you still there?"

"Yeah, yeah. Are you really asking me on a date? Are you interested in me now?"

"No!" Angelica instantly denied it. "I just need your help. I want to know if he still cares for me the least."

"Oh-oh, that's not a good idea. He might hunt me down. Why don't you just come to one of our gigs?"

"Gigs?"

"Yeah. Performances? There's a party later. My friends and I will perform there. I'll just message you the location."

"Okay."

"Bye. See you later."

"See you."

Angelica looked at the time on her phone, ran to her closet, and searched for something to wear. A minute later she was already in the bathroom having a shower.

She arrived at a restaurant and looked around. Angelica immediately saw Henry playing an acoustic guitar with his bandmates. They were performing a song while customers were dancing in the open space.

It was her first time hearing him sing. His voice was cold and soothing like the cold wind during the night. It perfectly fit the song he was singing.

"Wow, I didn't expect him to be such a great singer,," Angelica whispered to herself. She found an empty table and decided to have a seat. A waiter then came up to her and asked for her order.

Reading the menu, she asked for a seafood platter and Iced tea.

She watched the band playing jazz and it gave a romantic vibe. Personally, Angelica loved jazz so she was enjoying their performance.

An hour later, their gig came to an end. Henry saw her table and approached her with his friends. "Hey, Angel!"

"Hey,"

"Oooh. Is she your girlfriend?" asked the pianist. She looked at Angelica and wiggled her eyebrows.

"We're just friends, Hannah." Henry defended.

"And that's where relationships begin," the double bass player said.

Henry ignored them and turned to her. "By the way, meet my friends. Hannah, Ensio, and Primo."

"Hi, I'm Ensio. Nice to meet you." The double bass player reached out his hand for a handshake.

Angelica accepted it, "Angelica. Nice to meet you too." She then turned to Primo, the one who played the trumpet. He gave her a short bob of acknowledgement.

"How's our performance?" Ensio asked.

"It's great. You were all wonderful."

"We are actually colleagues and if we're free, we do gigs as our hobby and at the same time an extra income," Henry told her.

"Wow, that's nice. When did you form your band?"

It was Hannah's turn to answer. "We're college friends studying the same course and eventually working at the Zamora Broadcast Station owned by Henry's family."

Angelica listened to their stories and had a great night. It was a good feeling to meet new friends and do new things.

Stalking his 'girlfriend's' social media account, Adrian saw a new post that Angelica was tagged in.

She was with the man she had dinner with and a new group of friends. He browsed the photos and saw a photo of Angelica where the guy was resting his arm over her shoulder.

Adrian clenched the phone in anger. Because of that, he unknowingly reacted to the photo by giving it a heart emoticon. He only got aware of what he did when he looked at the post again. "What?" He tried to remove his reaction but it couldn't be undone.

Standing up, he paced back and forth. "What do I do?" Adrian tried to undo the emoticon but nothing was happening. "What will she think now?"

Angelica stepped out of the bathroom wearing a robe with a towel covered in her hair. She sat on the bed, picked up the phone that was sitting there, and looked at her social media account.

There was a notification that popped out so she clicked it and read, 'Adrian Fernando loved your post'

"What?" She clicked on the notification and it led her to Henry's post of their photo. "Hah!" Angelica teared up. "Until when are you going to make me wait? Making me wait without any reassurance? I'm getting tired, Adrian." She mumbled to herself, snuffling a little.

"You're okay if I date someone else?! Then I'll just start attending blind dates from now on!"

Marching out of her room, she knocked on her father's study. "Come in."

"What is it? Do you need something?" Alexander looked surprised that his daughter visited her.

Set me up on blind dates!, she thought but she did not want to do things impulsively. "Nothing. Goodnight."

"Goodnight." It was unusual of her to do that.

Angelica came back to her room and changed into her pajamas before climbing on the bed. She opened the photo of her and Adrian, their faces stuck together and had wacky expressions.

She bit her lower lip holding back herself from breaking apart. Why is it so hard to love? Is it supposed to be like this? Angelica closed her eyes and said to herself, "You need to move on if nothing's happening. Don't waste your time and energy on him."

Dereck received a call from Jamaica on a Monday morning. "Hello?"

"Hi, Dereck?"

"Yeah?" He sounded surly.

"I-uh, are you available? I need to ask a favor from you."

"What is it?" Dereck yawned.

"Can you take care of Camila for a week?"

"I'm working. I'm not sure if I can look at her. How about Yaya Mel?"

"She went home to her province because her husband is sick. I've been bringing Camila to the hospital with me for the past week. We have a medical mission in Tarlac for three days."

"Should I pick her up there?"

"No, I'll just drop her off before going to work. I already packed her things. I'll drive her there now."

"Okay." He immediately stood up from bed and ran to the bathroom after ending the call.

"Hey!" Adrian exclaimed. He was supposed to go in but Dereck forestalled him and took a quick bath.

An hour later, Jamaica and Camila were outside his apartment door knocking. "Dereck? Dereck?"

Adrian opened the door for them. He looked surprised to see them standing there.

"Is Dereck there?" she asked.

"Uh, yeah," He opened the door wider, "come in." Adrian guided them to the living room. "You're Jamaica, right?"

Jamaica nodded.

"And you must be little Camila?" Adrian smiled at her. "Wait for a while, he's just changing his clothes." He picked up his clothes sitting on the counter and entered the bathroom.

Looking around Jamaica saw how simply the two had been living. There were only necessities and no accessories or decorations. The apartment had an open living room connecting to the dining room and kitchen. It also had a bathroom in between two bedrooms.

They heard a door open and instantly saw Dereck coming out of the room. He looked fresh with his newly combed hair, white cotton shirt, and navy terry shorts.

"Hey, Mister! Good morning!" Camila waved at him while holding a stuffed toy in her other hand.

"Good morning, Princess." Dereck smiled at their daughter while he simply glanced at Jamaica.

She averted her gaze and looked at other things.

"So, you have a medical mission?" He sat beside Camila resting his back on the seat.

"Yeah, it's just for three days but it might be extended. I already packed a week's clothes here in her backpack. There are some of her toys in the duffel bag." She turned to Camila. "Sweetheart, I'll leave you to Daddy now, okay?"

"Daddy?" Camila tilted her head in confusion.

Jamaica realized she had a slip of tongue and shyly glanced at Dereck. "I mean Mister." She stood up and headed to the door. "I'll go now. Give Mommy a hug and a kiss."

Camila stood up on the sofa and encircled her arms around her mother's neck embracing her tight. She then gave her sloppy kisses all over her face making Jamaica laugh. "Sweety, that's ticklish."

Watching them, Dereck heard her laughter for the first time after a long time. It made his heart skip a beat. No matter how much he wanted to deny it, only Jamaica had that effect on him.

"I love you, Mommy."

"I love you too, baby." Jamaica gave her one last hug before going outside. "Bye. I'll call you after work every day, okay?"

"Okay." Camila started jumping up and down on the couch. "Bye, Mommy!"

Dereck felt envious of their closeness. When will I get to hear them say that to me? Sighing, he turned to their daughter and asked, "Did you have breakfast, Princess?"

"I only had a banana."

"Do you want to eat with me?"

Camila nodded, smiling.

Suddenly, Adrian got out of the bathroom and ran to his bedroom wearing only a towel.

"Do you want to watch T.V.?"

"Yes please!" Dereck turned on the television and then went to the kitchen to cook.

Adrian came out of his bedroom wearing a suit and tie. "Dude, cook mine too."

"Don't eat. You're late already."

They heard the little girl giggle. So both of them glanced at her. "What's your name, Uncle?"

"Me?" Adrian walked to her and sat beside her. He stretched out his hand. "My name is Adrian. Nice to meet you."

Camila took his hand. "Nice to meet you too, Uncle Adrian."

"Hey, why are you calling him Uncle when you call me Mister?" Dereck complained.

Adrian laughed. "Well, I think she likes me more."

Dereck grouched. He was jealous so he did not prepare any breakfast for his roommate.

"I'll buy breakfast on my way to work," Adrian told him as he headed to the door. "Bye! Bye, kiddo!"

"Bye Uncle!" Camila waved goodbye while Dereck frowned at her.

"Princess, breakfast is ready."

The little girl ran to the dining table and climbed up the chair. She was kneeling on the seat and stared at the table. "Wow! Did you cook all this, Mister?"

There was fried chicken, bacon, eggs, rice, bread, fruits, and pancakes.

"Yes. Why?"

"All are my favorite."

"Really? That's also my favorite food. Do you have any other favorites?

"Hmm... Steak!"

"Does Mommy always prepare your meals?"

"No, Mommy rarely cooks food at home. She always cuts herself when she's holding a knife."

"Really?" I didn't know that. "Sit properly." Dereck placed the rice on her plate. "What do you want to eat?"

"Everything."

He laughed and placed one of each food on her plate.

Sitting down on the chair across from his daughter's chair, he watched her eat. Dereck rested his chin on his fist as he observed little Camila.

She looked a lot like him but the way she stared was like Jamaica. It was as if she was reading what was going on inside his mind.

"Mister, you won't eat?"

Dereck grabbed bread, bacon, and a banana and then started eating. A moment later he asked her. "Aren't you gonna call me Uncle too?"

"No."

"Why?"

"You're Mister. You can't be Uncle."

"Huh? I don't get it." Dereck sighed and stuffed his mouth with a slice of bread. How I wish she could call me Daddy.

Chapter 16

There was no scheduled rehearsal so Dereck brought Camila to a toy store. "What toys do you want to buy, Princess? Name it."

Camila's eyes gleamed in delight. "Really?" She jumped up and down before running around the shop. Peeking through the shelves, she asked again. "You sure you won't make me pay what I'll take?"

Dereck chuckled and shook his head. He himself looked around for the toys he wanted to buy for her. He chose puzzles, board games, and video games according to her liking.

When they came back home, the two of them played with all of the toys for the whole day. And when evening came, Camila was so sleepy she preferred to sleep than eat dinner.

"Mister, I'm sleepy."

"We need to eat dinner first."

"I don't want to eat." Her eyelids were getting heavy.

Dereck went to his bedroom and prepared his bed for her. "Princess, brush your teeth first. Do you need me to help you shower?

"No. I can do it. Mommy said I'm a big girl now." Camila stepped inside the bathroom to freshen up.

He went to the kitchen, poured her a glass of milk, and handed it to her when she came out of the bathroom. "Here, drink this before going to bed."

She took the glass and instantly finished it. "Thank you, Mister." Camila climbed up the bed, lay down, and stared at him. "Can you tell me a bedtime story?"

Dereck was still holding the empty glass when he sat at the side of the bed. "What story do you want to hear?"

"Anything. I'm not used to sleeping without hearing any stories. Mommy always tells me one."

"Hmm... Do you want to hear how I met the love of my life?"

"The love of your life?"

He nodded. "Yes, the woman I love."

"What happened?"

"It all began seven years ago," Dereck started. "I loved performing on stage so I joined the theater organization. That's where I met her."

"She was near the stage tying her soft wavy brown hair up into a messy bun before holding the paintbrush again to color some props. At the same time, she was giving instructions to the other students."

He tried to come near her but the drama and theater teacher coordinator, Mrs. Santos, was already calling their attention. "Everybody, can you please gather around now?"

She was standing on the stage. "Today, we have our freshmen orientation. Those who would like to join our organization, can you please have a seat here in front?"

The students, including Dereck, sat in the front rows of their school's theater. His glance kept turning to the lady who caught his attention.

"I will introduce to you the seniors who are heading the different departments of our org." One by one Mrs. Santos called the senior students and he was starting to get bored. He scratched his ear waiting for everyone to finish introducing themselves and giving an overview of the departments they were handling until she was the one standing.

She stood in front of the crowd with all seriousness and introduced herself. "Hi, my name's Jamaica. I'm one of the set designers and in charge of designing the stage for the different scenes of the play. If anyone wants to join our department, you're all very welcome."

Dereck got curious about her more so he joined their department. They had a per department meeting so everyone gathered in circles. Jamaica and the other set designers were behind the stage. Five men joined their group so she asked them one by one. The four were studying fine arts while Dereck was a Performing Arts student.

"Shouldn't you be in the actors' department? Why did you join here?"

He thought of an excuse. "Well, I wanted to learn more about creating the stage."

Her eyebrows were still knitted, not believing a word he said but she still nodded. "Alright. We have a play already that is scheduled three months later. We need to prepare early. There's a script available and the producer already gave instructions."

Dereck was just watching her.

"What happened then?" Camila asked, yawning.

"Since then we became close. We were inseparable." He was staring into space.

"Does it mean you're still with her? Why don't I see her here? She didn't become your wife?"

Dereck was utterly speechless. He couldn't bring himself to tell the truth. So he reversed the question instead. "What about you? Don't you want to meet your Daddy?"

She yawned again, her eyes getting heavier. "I already met him."

His eyes grew wide in shock and turned his head. "What?!" His daughter was already sleeping soundly. Does she know it's me or is she talking about a different daddy?

His thought was interrupted when he heard Adrian open the door with a key. So Dereck went out of his bedroom to open it and welcome him. "Dude. You came back early."

"Yeah. I can't concentrate well on my work. I'd rather rest first." Adrian walked straight to the couch and sat.

"You look really exhausted."

Adrian just stared at the ceiling thinking of the stupidity he did last night. "How do you ease a woman's anger?"

"Huh?" Dereck stared at him with a confused look.

"I accidentally did something and I think Angelica's angry. I know she is but I don't know what to do."

"It's easy. Just buy her flowers or chocolates. Every woman likes that."

Adrian looked at him with narrowed eyes. "I don't think she'll like that."

"Well, it's better to try than not to do anything. Do you know what she likes?"

"That's the problem. I like her but I realized I didn't know anything about her."

"Now's the time to start knowing her, don't you think? If her father sees your efforts, maybe he'll approve of you."

"I guess so." Adrian leaned on the couch and stared at the ceiling again.

"I think the real question is, what do you really feel about her?" Dereck's question made him ponder.

Stephen and the other hospital staff were already in Tarlac for the medical mission. They were carrying the medical equipment to the tent when he caught up beside Jamaica and asked. "Who's with Camila now? Is Yaya Mel staying for three days to take care of her?"

"No. I left her with Dereck."

He was surprised. "Are you sure you can leave her to him?"

"I don't have anyone I can ask for a favor because Yaya Mel went home. And I believe it's a good chance for them to get closer."

Stephen wanted to argue but he respected her decision. How could I not be happy if they were building a family for Camila? I really need to settle my feelings for her now, he thought.

Jamaica left Stephen and went ahead when his phone vibrated. He put down the container he was holding and took out his phone. He received a message from Rosette.

Hey Doc, how are you? I was looking for you here in the hospital but they said you're in Tarlac?

Instead of texting a reply, he dialed her number and she immediately answered. "Hello?"

"Rosette, we're here for the three-day medical mission. Did you drop by to buy your medicine?"

"Yeah. I just thought I'll see you before I go."

"Oh, okay. I'll just let you know when I'm back."

"Okay! See you soon! Bye, Doc!" Rosette ended the call even before he could say goodbye.

Stephen snickered, carrying the box again.

Meanwhile, Adrian was in the shower early morning still thinking about his next step. He wasn't able to sleep a wink at all last night. His tears ran down his cheeks as the water from the showerhead poured down his face.

He turned off the shower trying to calm himself. Adrian cried his heart out. What do I need to do to make them see that what I feel for her is true? A part of his mind said another thing. If that's through you should be doing something. But isn't it enough that I listened and respected her father's decision?

He was on the verge of breaking down. He was not yet confident to love Angelica the way they wanted him to do so.

After having a bath, Adrian immediately called the friend who invited him to work in Australia. "Hey, bro, is your invitation still valid?"

"Yeah. Have you decided to finally establish a career in Australia?"

"I need to get out of here."

"Huh? What do you mean?"

"Nothing."

"Okay. I'll get back to you after talking to my boss."

"Sure. Thanks."

"Thanks, man. I've gotta go now. Bye." Adrian finished putting on his work clothes before knocking at Dereck's door.

"Dereck?" He called but no one answered. "Dereck?" He knocked again but this time Adrian quietly turned the knob and opened the door. He saw Dereck sleeping with Camila in his arms. With a smile, he still went in to wake his friend by tapping his foot. "Hey, Dereck, wake up. You have a rehearsal today, right?"

Dereck sat up. "Huh?" His eyes were still closed then opened wide. "Oh, right!"

"I'll prepare breakfast. You better get ready now and wake Camila up."

Thirty minutes later, Dereck was already dressed in a white shirt and denim jeans while Camila was wearing a pink casual dress.

"Let's eat," Adrian told them as he set up the table and place the foods he cooked.

Dereck and Camila sat on the chairs on one side and Adrian sat opposite them. "Where are we going today, Mister?"

"I'll bring you to the theater where we practice for a play."

"What play?"

"It's something I wrote."

"I want to see it!"

"Okay. Then let's hurry." Dereck checked the time on his watch. "We only have an hour."

Adrian was eating slowly so he asked him. "Hey, aren't you late for work?"

"Ah, yes." He sounded unbothered if he was late. Adrian stood up without finishing his meal. "I'll be late."

"Okay. Take care."

"Bye." He stepped out of the apartment and headed to work.

On his way to the law firm, Adrian passed by a flower shop. Different kinds of flowers were displayed by the glass windows and everything looked beautiful. He remembered what Dereck said about giving Angelica flowers or chocolates to say sorry.

Entering the shop, he decided to buy her that bouquet of flowers. Her reaction would be his sign if he will continue going to Australia or not.

"Good morning, how can I help you?" said a tall and muscular man standing by the counter.

"I-uh wanted to buy a bouquet."

"For your girlfriend?"

"Y-yeah..."

"Did you quarrel?" the man asked again.

Adrian just bowed his head, nodding.

"So, you'll give this to apologize to her?"

"That's what I want to do. I'm not sure if she'll accept it."

The florist moved out behind the counter and looked for the flowers for his bouquet. "One of the best flowers to give our blue hyacinths, pink carnations, and white lilies of the valley." He showed the flowers to Adrian. "Do you want me to combine them all?"

"Sure." Adrian noticed the man was limping but he was not using any cane.

After a few minutes, the bouquet was ready. "Here you go."

"Thanks." He paid the florist before walking out. Adrian smelled it and smiled. Somehow it made him happy. I hope she likes this.

Instead of going straight to work, he hailed a taxi to Stephen Brown Hospital. This is now or never.

Adrian asked the receptionist where he could find Angelica.

"Hi sir, sorry, Nurse Angelica is not here. She's one of the nurses who went to Tarlac for the medical mission."

He felt his whole world shattered. He was staring blankly so the receptionist called his attention.

"Sir, are you alright?" Adrian left the bouquet on the counter and walked out of the hospital weakly.

"Sir! Your flowers! Sir!"

Looks like we never really matched our timing.

Chapter 17

"This is the theater, Princess. Have you been to one?" Dereck was holding Camila's hand while entering the auditorium.

"No. This is my first time," she answered.

They sat in the front row near the stage, and Rosette and the other actors noticed them.

"Direk!" Her gaze shifted to the little girl. "Hey, kid, nice to see you again."

"What are you doing here?" Camila frowned.

"I'm one of your father's actresses."

Dereck glared at Rosette so she immediately closed her mouth. "I mean his actress." She just pointed to him.

Camila looked up at him. "Ah, you mean Mister? So, you dance and sing?"

"Yes. Do you want me to show you?"

Dereck interjected. "Rose, stop picking a fight with the little girl."

"I'm not."

"Yeah, right. Is everyone here?"

"Yes. We've been warming up. We can start now."

"Okay. The show will be in two weeks so we only have a few days remaining. We'll have a technical rehearsal next week. If we'll be able to perfect this today, you can have a two days rest before the tech rehearsal."

"Yes, Direk."

"Let's start now." Dereck took out his script and focused his attention on the stage. He opened the walkie-talkie in his hand to give directions to the technical team. They're in charge of the lighting and changes in the set design.

Camila, sitting quietly beside him, watched how the play unfold right before her eyes. "Wow!" She whispered.

She was amazed by how great all the actors were, especially Rosette. I wish I can be like her when I grow up.

After the first run, they had a ten-minute break so Rosette sat beside her. "What do you think? Am I good?"

Camila bowed her head and nodded. "You can have him now. He's all yours."

"Huh?" Rosette looked at Dereck who had the same expression as her.

Camila's phone started ringing so she answered it immediately. "Hello, Mommy?"

"Hi, sweetheart, how are you?"

"I'm fine, Mommy. Mister brought me here to the theater."

"Really? Have fun, okay? I'll call later before you go to sleep."

"Okay, Mommy. I love you."

"Love you too, baby." Someone called Jamaica in the background. "I have to go now. Bye!"

"Bye-bye, Mommy!" Camila bagged her phone when Dereck asked her.

"What did your Mommy say?"

"She'll call later."

"Did she ask about me?"

"Nope."

Dereck sighed and that made Rosette laugh. "Are you giving up already, Direk? You haven't even courted Jamaica properly."

"You like my Mommy?" Camila asked, her wide eyes growing even bigger.

"Isn't it obvious, Princess?"

"Nope. And I think you should be asking for my approval first, Mister."

"So, can I court your Mommy?"

"No!" Camila smirked. She leaned on the chair while her arms were crossed over her chest.

Rosette laughed at their cute interaction. Like father, like daughter, she thought. They're both playful.

Jamaica pocketed her phone after the phone call with her daughter. She couldn't help but smile knowing that Camila and Dereck were starting to get close. She continued eating her lunch quickly so she could get back to work.

She noticed Stephen was eating a sandwich in a corner and she decided to walk toward him. "Hey," Jamaica nudged him lightly on the side.

"Hi," he said, avoiding her gaze. "I'll go back to work now," Stephen said as soon as he finished his food.

Jamaica watched him leave in worry. "Is he sick?"

They had been serving the indigent people in Tarlac for a whole day. It was around six in the evening when they were traveling from the mountains back to the city to have a rest.

The medical team arrived at the hotel reserved for them. Jamaica and Angelica stayed in one room. "I'll have a shower first," Angelica told her.

"Okay," Jamaica rested her back on the pillow and dialed Camila's number for a video call.

"Hello, Mommy," Camila's face appeared on her screen.

"Hello, baby. Did you eat dinner?"

"Yes. Mister cooked Omurice. It was very delicious."

"Wow! Mister is a great cook, right?"

"Yes!"

Dereck was in the kitchen washing the dishes when he heard Camila talking on the phone with Jamaica. He turned off the faucet and walked behind the little girl to listen to their conversation.

"Wow! Mister is a great cook, right?" Jamaica said. He could see the dark circles under her eyes.

"Yes!" Camila giggled. "Mister is better than you Mommy."

"Ouch. It looks like you love Mister more than me now."

Camila giggled again. "Mommy you're not cute."

"Hey, you like teasing me huh?" Jamaica had a smile on her tired face. "Sleep early, sweetheart. Mommy's going to rest now. We still have to wake up early tomorrow."

"Okay, Mommy."

"Bye, sweetie. I love you! Mwah!"

"I love you too, Mommy! Goodnight!" Camila waved good-bye before ending the call.

"Your Mommy looks exhausted," Dereck commented, startling her.

"Mister!"

"I'm just watching you two." He sat beside her. "Take a shower now so you can go to bed."

Camila followed his instruction leaving her phone sitting on the couch. Dereck got curious and checked the gallery. There he saw countless photos of the mother and daughter. Most were photos with Stephen so he got jealous and wanted to delete them. Instead, he opened the camera and took selfie photos of himself.

For the remaining two days, Dereck and Camila got closer than before.

They were in a cake shop buying her favorite cake when the cashier asked her. "Hey, pretty girl, is he your daddy?"

Camila and Dereck exchanged glances. He was already expecting her answer and it surprised him when she replied, "Yes. Isn't he handsome? People said we look alike."

"Yes." The cashier was looking seductively at Dereck and Camila was glaring at her.

"Hey, miss. My Daddy is not available, okay? Mommy will get mad." She held Dereck's hand. He was too stunned to say anything.

The cashier laughed at Camila's response. "I guess you really love your daddy, huh?"

"Yes. He loves me and Mommy only."

"That's so sweet. Anyway, here's your cake." Dereck took out his wallet to get cash for the cake before taking it.

"Thank you."

"You're welcome, sir. Have a good day!"

Camila dragged Dereck outside the store, still looking grumpy. She doesn't want her father getting attention from other women.

"Princess, wait. Where are we going?"

"Home."

"Home? My house is this way." Dereck stopped in his tracks and pointed the other way.

"No. Let's go home." She started wailing.

Dereck tried calling Jamaica hoping she was not busy. Thankfully she answered. "Yes, is there any problem, Dereck?"

"It's Camila."

"Why?! What happened?!"

"She's fine but she's crying asking me to go home."

"Go home?"

"Yup. At your house."

"Why?"

"I don't know."

"Are you alright if you go home with her? She has a spare key inside her bag."

"I'm okay with that. I'll message you when we get there."

"Okay," Jamaica sighed. "Dereck, thanks." There was a long pause before she talked again. "I'll reach home around 12 midnight."

"No worries," he said. "You go back to work. Sorry for interrupting you."

"It's okay. Bye now. Don't forget to text me."

"Yeah. Bye. Take care." Dereck ended the call and went to the bedroom where Camila was sulking. "Princess? Your Mommy said we can go home. I'll just pack a few of my things then we'll leave."

"Really?" Her face lit up, she ran to Dereck then jumped to him, and hugged him tightly. "Yehey!"

Dereck chuckled. One moment she's angry, then she'll be sad the next time she's happy. She's so hard to understand.

After an hour of travel, Dereck and Camila reached Sta. Inez's residence. She was so excited to be back home with her father.

"Do you want to eat again or do you want to sleep?"

"Sleep! Tell me a story again."

"Okay. Change into your pajamas. Is there a guest room I can use?"

"Just sleep with me in our bedroom, Mister." She opened their room door and invited him inside.

He was amazed to see that it was filled with their photos and the bed was right beside the window overlooking the wonderful view outside.

It was Jamaica's old room as far as he remembered. They used to hang out there when they were planning and designing the stage for the plays. All the memories they shared came flashing back at him.

"Mister?"

"Huh?"

"I'll just change my clothes." Camila was holding her pajamas and ran to the bathroom. Dereck, on the other hand, texted Jamaica that they were already home.

Minutes later, she was ready to sleep and Dereck was telling her a new story, making her fall asleep.

He caressed her cheek before going out of the room to drink a glass of water. Dereck was having a sip of the drink when he heard the front door open. The moment he turned around he and Jamaica instantly locked gazes at each other.

Jamaica was sent by a taxi in front of their house. She quietly opened the gate and carried her bags to the front door. When she found the key of the door among her other keys, she finally opened it and kicked her bags inside.

Her eyes glanced around the living room and fixated her gaze on Dereck who was standing by the kitchen counter as he drank water. She wanted to run to him to hug him, kiss him, and never let him go.

Jamaica could see his gaze was darker than the room. It was the same look he had that day.

She stepped back but she already felt she was trapped and unable to move.

Dereck slowly took his steps towards her like a predator who caught its prey.

Their breaths were only heard. Without asking or saying a thing, he grabbed her neck and claimed her lips fully and hungrily.

She wanted to push him away but all her strength was being sucked out of her. Jamaica began kissing back, yearning for him after all the years they had been apart. Her arms circled behind his neck pulling him closer.

Both of them were panting, gasping for air. She realized the foolishness she had done so she immediately removed her arms from him as if she was burned. "I-I... I'll go up now," Jamaica whispered, avoiding his gaze.

Dereck grabbed her arm. "J..."

"Let's talk tomorrow, D." Jamaica went upstairs leaving her bags by the door, blocking the way.

Sighing, he took the bags and placed them beside the couch. He went back to the kitchen and drank colder water. "What did you just do, Dereck?" He wanted to bang his head on the wall.

Getting inside their room, Jamaica searched for comfortable clothes to wear and headed to the bathroom. She wanted to cool herself down.

Later she stepped out refreshed. Jamaica climbed up from the bed and hugged Camila tight. "I love you, sweetie," she whispered and kissed her cheek. She finally closed her eyes and went to sleep.

Dereck went inside the room around two in the morning after giving thought to a lot of things. He wanted to sleep in the other rooms but all were locked so he had no choice but to sleep with them.

Since Camila was in the middle and Jamaica was on the left side, Dereck lay down on the right side of their daughter. He stared at the ceiling and then turned to face Camila. I love you, Princess.

The following day, Dereck's arm was resting on Jamaica's waist. He was caressing her back thinking it was still Camila.

Jamaica started getting ticklish of what he was doing so she grabbed his hand and removed it from her back. She wanted to sleep in since it was her day off.

Turning around, she moved away from him but he pulled her closer to him and hugged her securely. "Let's sleep a little longer. I wasn't able to sleep 'til four."

"Mommy!" Camila opened the door wide. "Papi and Mamita are here!"

Jamaica instantly sat up. "What?!"

Chapter 18

Dereck tiptoed inside the room and quietly climbed up beside their daughter. He stared at Jamaica and Camila all night long. He placed his arm around Camila and held her to sleep.

He felt Camila turn around, moving out of bed. He opened an eye and peeked at his wristwatch seeing that it was just six in the morning. "Ugh," he complained when he saw Jamaica was sound asleep facing him. A smile crept on his lips while naughtily putting his arm on her waist. It seemed like he had woken her up since she removed his hand behind her and turned her back on him.

Pulling her closer he said, "Let's sleep a little longer. I wasn't able to sleep 'til four." Dereck was waiting for her to remove his hand again instead she held it.

Dereck tried to have a look at her face but he couldn't see her expression at all. "What you did last night, do you mean it?"

"What do you mean?"

"Are you serious or you're making me have false hope?"

"How could you think like that?"

Jamaica turned to face him. "You can't blame me. You haven't proven anything. Do you really love me? Do you even like me? Or you do just feel obliged to be with me because of Camila?"

"I-I,"

"I'm not expecting something but I also don't want to hope so I'm drawing a clear line here. The line I wasn't able to draw seven years ago. Don't make me guess what our relationship is. I'm tired of trying to figure out what we are." Jamaica sat up and was about to get up when Camila opened the door widely.

"Mommy, Papi and Mamita are here!" She was smiling from ear to ear.

"What?!" Jamaica glanced at the curious Dereck. Alarmed, she jumped out of the bed, pulled Camila inside the room, and closed the door, locking it.

"You need to hide," she said to Dereck. "Mom and Dad can't know you're here."

"Why? I want to meet them. I. NEED. TO. MEET. THEM." He looked straight into her eyes.

Jamaica was so worried because she hadn't told Camila the truth yet.

He jumped out of bed, grabbed Jamaica's hand, and dragged her out of the room. They walked down the stairs and saw the elderly couple sitting on the couch.

"Jamaica!"

"Sweetheart!"

Jamaica pulled her hand out of Dereck's grasp and ran down the stairs to meet her parents. "Mom, Dad!" She hugged them and then kissed their cheeks. However, their eyes were fixated on Dereck who was standing behind their daughter while holding Camila's hand.

"Young lady, I think you've got some explaining to do," Joselito told his daughter.

Stephen was standing on his bedroom balcony stretching his arms up and to the sides. For the past three days of their stay at Tarlac, he had constant communication with Rosette and it made him know her more. Surprisingly, they had a lot of common interests and at the same time, they had huge differences. But one thing is for sure, he's starting to have feelings for her.

He went back inside his bedroom and reached out for his phone that was sitting on top of the bed. Stephen opened his previous conversation with Rosette and typed a message.

To: RosetteHey, are you available at 7 p.m.? I have something to tell you.He was startled when she instantly replied back.From: RosetteYeah, sure. Where will we meet?

To: RosetteLet's meet at McDonald's near your place. I'll go there later.

From: RosetteOkay. See you later.

His dog, Chopper, a black Shi Tzu, circled around his feet asking for food. "Hey, buddy, are you hungry?" Stephen played with him. "Come on." He was smiling from ear to ear that his jaws and cheeks began aching. He felt nervous and excited at the same time.

Rosette squealed inside her room making her mother, Rowena, come upstairs and barged in to see her. "What's happening? Are you okay?"

She smiled awkwardly. "Yeah, Mom!" Her voice was high-pitched in overjoy.

Rowena shook her head in disbelief. She couldn't understand her daughter most of the time. "Come down now and help me in the restaurant."

"Okay! By the way Mom, can I go out around 7 p.m.? A friend from the theater was asking to meet me."

"Okay. No problem." She waited for her mother to leave the room and close the door then she immediately locked it.

Rosette breathed deeply, inhaled, and exhaled, before jumping up and down, dancing around her room like a crazy person. She had a hunch about what Stephen would tell her. "He's gonna tell me he likes me!" She whispered to herself and squealed as quietly as she could.

Calming down, she looked in the mirror of her vanity table and saw how flushed she looked. Her cheeks were so hot she stood in front of the electric fan to cool her face.

"Why are you here, Mr. Sy? Have you and my daughter had a talk already?" Joselito asked Dereck.

They were in the study including Jamaica. Camila was left with her grandmother, Claudine, playing.

"She told me that I'm Camila's dad."

"And do you believe that?"

Dereck got confused. "What do you mean, Uncle, I mean, Sir?"

"I am asking if you believe that the child is yours."

"Y-yeah..."

"Are you sure about that?"

He was getting more confused and at the same time intimidated because of her father's gaze. I'm sure, he thought, but why can't I answer?

Joselito looked disappointed since he was not able to give any answer. Jamaica had to step in. "Dad, why are you asking like that?"

He looked at her daughter with the same expression on his face. "I want to make sure he's not confused about what's happening and I want to know what he truly thinks about you. Is that a bad thing?"

She sighed walking out of the room.

Dereck understood her father. He just wanted to protect her, especially after what happened to them seven years ago. "Sir," he cleared his throat, "it is my dream to have a complete family because growing up, I had no one beside me. Until now, I still couldn't believe that we have Camila. I want to be with them and be part of their life from now on."

"How will you do that? Does Camila know you're her father?"

"Not yet. I want to gain their trust first, Sir, and I want to date your daughter with marriage in mind." Dereck stared straight into Joselito's eyes full of sincerity and determination.

"Very well. Don't forget that I'm watching you. Make my daughter cry again and you won't get to see them ever again."

"Yes, Sir."

"You don't have to call me like that. Just call me Uncle Lito again like before." Dereck smiled, nodding.

Going out of the study, the two men went down and saw the ladies setting the table. Dereck called their attention by bidding farewell. "I'll get going now."

"Why don't you eat breakfast with us?" Auntie Claudine told him with a warm smile on her face.

"Yes, Daddy. Eat with us," said Camila. She ran to him, grabbed his hand, and dragged him to the table.

They were all too stunned after hearing that she called him 'Daddy'.

Dereck exchanged glances with Jamaica who just shrugged her shoulders.

Joselito and Claudine sat down on their chairs and asked the kid. "Do you know that he's your Daddy?"

"Yes!"

"Sweetheart, why didn't you tell me?" Jamaica asked.

"You never asked me, Mommy. I also thought you were keeping it a secret, that's why I didn't say anything."

After the meal, Joselito and Claudine played with their granddaughter in the living room while Dereck and Jamaica were washing the dishes. "How did she know that I'm her dad?"

"I don't know."

"If she already knew, then why is she calling me 'Mister'?"

"Beats me. Maybe she's just messing with you?" His face immediately darkened but it only made her laugh. "You look ugly."

"What? Say that again!" He started poking her on the sides making her squeal.

"Hey, Mom and Dad can hear us! Stop!" Jamaica was stepping away from him.

Their little play was interrupted when Dereck's phone rang in his pocket. He pulled it out and answered, "Hello, Adrian? What's up?"

"Hey, bro. I have something to tell you. When are you coming home?"

"I'll go home today."

"Okay. Talk to you later." Dereck noticed Jamaica distanced herself and continued washing the dishes. He stood beside her again and said, "By the way, I have something to give you."

She only looked up at him. He took out four tickets for the play he was directing. "The show is on Saturday next week. I hope you can come. You can also bring Uncle, Auntie and Camila with you if you like. That's just a one-time play and there won't be any run after."

"Okay. I'll check my schedule that day."

"That's great." His smile was from ear to ear. Dereck wanted to hold her but he didn't know where to put his hands. "I'll go home now."

"I'll take you to the gate." Jamaica offered and the both of them went to the living room. "Mom, Dad, Dereck's leaving."

"Okay, take care, son." Claudine said while Joselito nodded his head.

"No Daddy!" Camila shouted, surprising them again. "Don't go!" She cried.

Dereck looked at everyone before crouching down to match her height. "I'll just meet with Uncle Adrian and get some clothes. Stop crying. Do you want to be ugly?"

Camila cried harder. He laughed, patting his daughter's head and wiping her tears away. "Do you want to go with me?"

The little girl nodded while wiping the snot on her nose.

"Can I bring her?" He asked Jamaica.

"Sure. Just come back early."

"Yes, Ma'am!" Dereck said and their daughter copied him.

Waking up from an afternoon nap, Rosette checked the time on her phone. "Shit! It's already 6:30 in the evening?! How long have I been asleep?"

She immediately stood up and rummaged through her closet for a nice set of clothes. Standing up in front of her full-length mirror, she tried matching blouses or shorts to her skirts or pants. "Ugh, why can't I find anything nice?"

Her eyes noticed the skirt she had been keeping for special occasions. It was an orange floral pleated skirt. Rosette took it and searched for her square-neck white crop top that could go well with her white sneakers.

Taking a five-minute shower, she then fixed herself up. Rosette ponytailed her long hair using a scrunchie with panda designs. It was given to her by someone she doesn't remember. She had one last look at herself in front of the mirror before going out of her bedroom.

The fast-food restaurant was only five blocks away from their house so instead of riding a tricycle she preferred to walk. Doing that made their "date" more exciting and nerve-wracking for her. And she loved that. Boring stuff doesn't suit her.

Rosette took her time walking, thinking and debating what to do, and what to say, calming herself to not expect too much because most of the time when you have high expectations, disappointments hurt the most.

She was the first one to arrive at McDonald's and went straight to the second floor. Glancing around, she sat in the farthest corner away from most of the customers. It was like a private table. Rosette sat down on one of the chairs and texted Stephen.

To: Doc Stephen

Hey Doc, I'm already here in McDo.

From: Doc Stephen

Okay. Just wait for me. I'm on my way now.

Waiting, she clasped her hands together. The beating of her heart was becoming louder and louder. Whoo, Rosette, calm down, she said in her mind. She distracted herself by playing mobile games.

She barely noticed that a few minutes had passed. When she looked up to where the stairs were, Rosette saw Stephen glancing around until their eyes met.

Both of them smiled at each other and that was already the happiest day for her because she knew that moment something between them changed.

Chapter 19

Dereck turned off his car's engine and unbuckled his seatbelt along with Camila's who was sitting beside him in the passenger's seat. "Let's go."

He got out of the car and ran to the other side to open the door for his daughter. He carried her into his arms and entered the building.

Knocking on the apartment door, Dereck waited for Adrian to open it. "Hey, bro."

"I thought it was someone else. You have a key right?"

"Sorry, I'm carrying her and you're in." He put Camila down. "So, what is it you want to talk about?"

Adrian pushed his glasses back on the bridge of his nose and said, "I'm leaving for Australia."

"What?! Already?" Dereck followed him to the kitchen.

"I'll leave after watching your play."

"Why?" Adrian just stared at him. "Make me understand. Why do you need to go abroad? You have a fine career here. Do you want to have this apartment all on your own?"

"No, it's not like that, bro." He looked troubled.

"Is it because of Angelica?"

"It's me. I'm the problem in our relationship." Adrian looked away.

"I know and you're running away." Dereck sat on one of the stools, sighing. "One thing I'll say, dude. When you're ready, face your problems head-on. Don't be scared. I can tell this now because I've been there. Think about things thoroughly so you won't regret any life choices you make. Weigh things so if ever you have regrets you could choose the thing you'll regret less.

"That's all I want to say. I'm not a fan of long talks so I'll stop here. By the way, I'll be living with Jamaica and Camila from now on. I came to get some of my things."

Adrian didn't seem like listening but he was. He was happy for Dereck. Deep in his heart, he wishes them the best so he smiled but it didn't reach his eyes.

"You know what, you don't need to pretend in front of me." Dereck left him to bag some clothes. After a few minutes, he came out of the room with a large duffel bag and a backpack. "Let's go, Princess." He glanced at Adrian who was still sitting by the dinner table, staring blankly. "We'll be going now."

Camila got off of the couch and ran to Adrian. She pulled his arm to reach his face and kissed him on the cheek. "Bye-bye, Uncle Adrian." She smiled before running towards Dereck.

"Hey, how come you're kissing him and I'm not?"

The little girl just giggled.

"Bye, dude. Just call me, okay?" Dereck said then left.

Adrian never felt so lonely in his life. When he was a child, it did not bother him much that he was an orphan because he never felt small or insignificant. But with Angelica, there was that feeling, that he needed to have something more. He needed to become someone else.

He was scared that if he became what Angelica's father wanted, he might lose himself.

Stuck in the traffic, Stephen checked his wristwatch. It was already fifteen minutes past their appointment time. It would take him at least thirty minutes to arrive at the restaurant.

He texted Rosette hoping he wouldn't be stood up.

To: Rosette

Hey, I'm stuck in traffic. Are you still good?

From: Rosette

I"m already hungry. T_T

To: Rosette

Just wait for me. I'll be there soon.

From: Rosette

Okay. :)

He reached McDonald's and parked his car nicely before turning off the engine and getting off. Stephen stared at the building nervously. "Whoo. You can do this." He said to himself.

His hands were trembling as he grabbed the glass door handle and pushed it open. Upon entering the restaurant, his eyes immediately searched for Rosette. She was not on the ground floor so he went straight to the second floor half running and half walking.

Stephen stood at the end of the stairs searching for her. He turned around and saw she was sitting at the farthest corner behind him.

Their eyes instantly met and he tensed. It was his first time feeling like that. Even though he liked Jamaica, he felt comfortable around her but when he's around Rosette, it was different.

She was looking at him with a huge smile on her face. Stephen slowly approached her with every nervous step. He could only smile back since he was afraid his voice might crack. Breathing deeply, he calmed himself before speaking. "I'll go down to order. What do you want to eat?"

"I'll have what you'll eat."

"O-okay. I'll j-just go down." He couldn't help but feel weird. He hasn't said anything yet to Rosette but it felt like they were already in a new phase of their relationship or whatsoever.

Stephen stood in line and waited for his turn. "What is your order, sir?"

"I'll have two double burgers with large fries and a large soda."

The cashier repeated his order as she punched it into the POS machine. "That would be four hundred pesos."

He handed her a five hundred peso bill and the cashier gave a change of one hundred pesos before processing his order.

Seconds later, the cashier handed him the tray of food. "Thank you, sir."

"Thank you." Stephen carried the tray upstairs to their table. "Here you go." He said to Rosette.

"Yehey!" She immediately took a few pieces of fries, stuffing her mouth. He was just watching her, enjoying every second of their "date".

Rosette has a keen sense and noticed he was staring at her. "What are you looking at? Is there something on my face?" She touched her cheeks.

Stephen chuckled, shaking his head.

"Why aren't you eating then?"

Stephen whispered, "I'm too nervous to eat."

"Why? Because we're eating together? We are always eating together." She said with a laugh. "By the way, why did you ask to meet?"

He exhaled loudly. His voice was trembling. "Here it goes," It's all or nothing, he thought. Stephen looked directly into her eyes and said, "I like you."

Fireworks display. Roller coaster ride. Palpitation due to excessive consumption of coffee. That's what Rosette was feeling. The mixed emotions of hearing your "crush" confess were too overwhelming to contain. But she couldn't let him see that. So, she acted cool and calm.

She cleared her throat and smirked. "Well, I like you too."

His eyes widened in surprise. He already knew she liked him because he could always feel it. But for her to say it so casually like that. Being young sure is different, he thought.

"So... is this the start of our first day?"

"No, you should ask my mom first." Rosette laughed then took a bite of her burger.

"O-okay."

"Eat now. You're so pale I thought you'd pass out."

He smiled and grabbed his burger to eat. He leaned on his chair and released a breath he didn't realize he was holding.

Staring at him, she gave him the sweetest smile she could and it was so infectious. Stephen took a bite of his burger to hide the smile on his face. Even so, his eyes were reflecting the happiness he was feeling.

They spent their date asking each other personal questions.

"By the way, I want to give you this." Rosette grabbed her black mini backpack to get a ticket. "We have a musical play this coming Thursday. I hope you can watch it since it will only be a one-time run."

"Okay. I'll try to free my schedule." He took the ticket and placed it in his wallet. When he looked back at her, Stephen noticed how tired her eyes were. "I think we should go home now. You look really sleepy."

"I'm just tired of the rehearsals," she replied, yawning.

He stood up. "Come on, I'll take you home."

She stood up and went down the stairs first followed by Stephen. He noticed the scrunchie she was using and it was the scrunchie he gave her ten years ago. "Where did you get this?" He touched it.

Rosette touched the scrunchie with the palm of her hand. "This? Someone gave it to me when I was a kid."

They reached the parking lot, got inside the car, and continued their conversation. "Do you remember who that was?"

"I think it was a nurse. But I vaguely recall."

Unconsciously, Stephen pouted his lips. She glanced at him and asked. "Why did you ask?"

"Nothing."

"All I know is that he was my first love."

For the second time, Stephen was surprised. "What?!"

Rosette glanced back at him from looking outside the window. "I said he was my first love. Are you jealous?" She smiled mischievously and poked his side.

"Hey, stop!" Stephen said. "We might get into an accident if you don't stop."

Fifteen minutes later, Stephen stopped the car in front of Rowena's. "So, I'll just text you when I get home," he said.

Rosette nodded but she did not get out yet. She lowered her head, biting her lower lip as she waited for the right time to execute what she had in mind.

Without any warning, she quickly kissed his cheek and then opened the door to get out. Rosette smiled, waved goodbye to him, and ran inside the restaurant. She left him staring blankly.

Stephen could only watch her in shock. He touched the cheek where he felt her lips. His heart raced. "Is this what dating feels like?"

He got home with a light heart as if he was on cloud nine. He couldn't stop smiling his jaw was already aching. Massaging his cheeks he told himself, "Stephen, stop smiling."

Chapter 20

There were two actors on the stage. The man, Israel, was standing in a circle on one side while Rosette, who was in the character of Celina, was on the other side.

Israel stepped foot on Celina's side and started dancing elegantly around her. Her eyes were filled with amusement following his every move.

When she stretched out her arm to reach out to him, he stood outside of her circle and went back to his.

Carefully thinking of her action, Celina bravely stepped out of her place to Israel's side and tapped his shoulder.

He turned around smiling at her. Israel didn't expect she would boldly approach him and give him the warmest smile he had ever seen.

She was waiting for him to dance and ask for her hand but he didn't. He wasn't. Her shoulders fell. Celina got tired of waiting so she went back to her place.

A while later, Israel was on her side of the stage again, inside the circle. Now, he was finally asking her to dance.

However, he was not asking for her hand but he wanted a partner for Cha Cha.

That lasted for days that turned into months that turned into years. Because she was not the only one he was asking to dance. He thought that would be the easiest way to find his match.

Israel had been asking a lot of women. And what's frustrating about that was he was asking for their hand. How can she get angry or jealous when the two of them don't have a relationship?

One time, Celina gathered her courage and went to Israel's side full of determination. Wearing red tango visite with her best smile, she bravely asked his hand for a dance. A dance of love — tango.

Israel was interested in her but not the way she was with him. Or maybe, he felt the same way. However, Celina was one of a kind.

Desire came to him so he took her hand, pulled her into an embrace, and swept her off her feet. His long fingers were sitting comfortably on her lower back.

The actors were looking only at each other's eyes as they moved across the stage. His arm was around her waist, tightly holding her closer. His stare and his actions were aggressive. One that Celina hadn't seen before so she got nervous.

It wasn't time to have second thoughts. It was a once-in-a-lifetime chance to be with him. Instead of getting scared, she finished the dance with Israel as the music ended with one final pose. A kiss.

The whole auditorium turned dark and came in a voice. It was a man's cry. He was weeping his heart out.

A spotlight opened, focused on Israel who was standing at the center. His face was covered in tears.

He opened his mouth and started singing.

How could you leave? How could you leave me behind?

Without even a single glance my heart was broken twice

Why couldn't you wait? For my feelings to be the same

Why couldn't you wait? Until we are brought by fate

Let me love you now my precious friend Celina

Tears streamed down Jamaica's cheeks and she doesn't know why. "Mommy, why are you crying?"

She immediately wiped her tears away. "I'm not crying, sweetheart." Jamaica smiled at her daughter before turning back her attention to the play.

Seeing you again was the most unexpected

A dream that turned into reality

For someone who has been loving you since day one

That later realized when you were already gone

Let me love you still my only woman Celina

It went dark again then the lights from the stage opened revealing Rosette. She was now different. A new woman. Stronger. Braver. Colder.

Israel entered the stage, trying to approach her but no matter how hard he took steps he couldn't seem to move out of his place. He was stuck.

She was going away, he couldn't catch up to her. His arm was reaching out to hold her. Sadly, he failed to grasp her hand. "Celina!" Israel wept and whispered, "I love you..." He kneeled down, hopeless.

The red curtain then a spotlight focused on Dereck as he walked up the stage. He stood at the center with a mic in his hand. "Good evening ladies and gentlemen, I created this play to dedicate it to someone special to me. At first, I didn't realize her importance but as years passed by it turned out that she was someone," he paused, "the woman I couldn't bear to lose in my life. So tonight, in front of all of you, I want to take this opportunity and ask her."

He tried looking within the crowd, specifically where Jamaica and Camila were sitting. The seats were empty. Where are they?

Jamaica was carrying Camila and they were already at the lobby walking out of the theater. She couldn't hold her tears any longer. Does he expect me to understand him just like that? After lifting me high and leaving me hanging all alone? Why do I have to be the one who understands? I'm getting tired! Why can't someone see that I'm hurting?

She immediately placed Camila inside the passenger's seat and then got in the driver's seat. Biting her lower lip, Jamaica covered her face with both hands and sobbed.

Her daughter gave her a hug. "Mommy, don't cry." She patted her mother's head which made Jamaica cry harder.

"Oh, Sweetie," she circled her arms around Camila.

Meanwhile, Adrian was sitting on the balcony and caught a glimpse of Angelica sitting at the orchestra. He stood up and passed by the other people to get to the lobby.

A little later, many were going out so Adrian kept waiting and looking for Angelica. "Where is she?" He whispered.

Angelica was briskly walking towards the exit, blending in with the mob. "Angelica!" She heard someone call her. "Angelica!" She recognized that it was Adrian's voice and tried to run away.

Getting out of the building, she sped up her steps. "Wait!" He grabbed her left arm after running up to her.

Angelica snapped at him, glaring. "What now?!"

"Let me explain."

"There's nothing to talk about, Adrian."

"No! We have many things to discuss." Seeing his face angered her. She scoffed. Here we go again. I'm already tired of all of this. "Let's stop seeing each other. Though, that's what we've been doing. Let's just end all of this, Adrian. Don't contact me."

"No! Listen to me!" He held her shoulders.

"Stop doing things as you please!" Her voice broke. "Why do you come and go whenever you like? You haven't even asked me how I feel. You're not the only one involved in this. It's the two of us."

Adrian was shocked. He knew her as someone patient, someone kind and understanding. She doesn't even know how to get angry. But I guess being with me is a bad thing. So instead of fighting for what he wanted, for what his heart wanted, he let her go.

He turned around defeated, going his own way and Angelica did the same. She wanted to look back but her pride could not handle it anymore. No more just me giving way, adjusting, letting him make me miserable like this. I want him to fight for us. But if he will always raise the white flag then I guess there's no real us.

They parted hearts torn and broken more than they"ll ever be. Their relationship ended even before it could begin.

The skies cried with them that night.

Looking for the dressing room, Stephen was holding a bouquet of colorful daisies. He found a room with an open door and saw the actors removing their makeup in front of the mirror and some changing clothes.

He knocked on the door to make his presence known. All turned in his direction. "Doc! What are you doing here?" Rosette stood up from her seat to approach him. She was still in her costume and makeup which made her much more beautiful, now that he'd seen her close.

Stephen revealed the flowers he was hiding behind his back. "Congratulations."

Her co-actors started teasing her. She only smiled, smelling the flowers. "Thank you for this." She then gave it back, "What are you doing here?"

"I wanted to treat you to a meal. To celebrate."

"Really?!" Her eyes glowed up. Stephen chuckled. If she's a rabbit, her ears would probably be clapping, he thought.

She went back inside the room to get her clothes and stepped in the changing room. In a pink hoodie and chiffon square pants, she came out and grabbed her things. "Let's go." Rosette told Stephen. She turned around and said good-bye to her co-workers.

They were heading their way out of the theater talking about what to eat. "What do you want to have?" he asked.

"Hmmm... I want to have a large meal." Rosette kept smelling the flowers as they walked.

"Don't eat too much. It's not good for you."

"Yes, Doc!" She exclaimed, smiling.

Dereck immediately left the place after the play. Instead of going home to the Sta. Inez's residence, he decided to go to their apartment. Adrian heard him enter but he did not bother greeting him. He was drowning himself in a beer in hopes of getting drunk.

Seeing him like that, Dereck went straight to the kitchen and opened the refrigerator to grab his own beer. He then came back to the living room and sat across from Adrian.

"What happened to you? Did you watch the play?"

"Yeah. I saw Jamaica leaving in the middle of the play."

He wanted to curse but he just drank it away. "Why do you look like you'll die?" he asked Adrian again.

"Angelica ended everything."

"Good to know. Finally, she should've done that a long time ago." Dereck bobbed his head.

Adrian threw a throw pillow and cursed at him. He was known to be a good kid who was so innocent and kind. It was a rare moment for Dereck to hear him, that's why he laughed.

They laughed and then had a long sigh. "I can't believe we'll be ruining our relationships." Dereck stared at the ceiling holding his third can of beer.

"Hey, we don't have any relationships with them. You're not Jamaica's boyfriend."

"But I'm the father of her daughter!"

"Yeah, yeah. Saying and acknowledging you are Camila's father, doesn't mean she needs to be in a relationship with you or be involved with you. Both of you can still support Camila as her parents without being a couple.

Dereck clenched his fist in anger, crushing the can of beer.

"By the way, my flight is tomorrow at noon. Are you going to drive me to the airport?"

"Do you want me to?"

"It would be good since no one would really care if I leave." Adrian choked remembering how he and Angelica parted. He removed his sunglasses and quietly removed the tears in the corners of his eyes. I don't have the right to shed a tear. Everything is my fault. He breathed deeply but his chest only tightened. He was in deep pain so he opened another can of beer and chugged it all down.

"Don't drink too much. You said your flight is tomorrow." Dereck removed the can from his hand and started cleaning up. "Go to sleep. Let's just sleep. Drinking won't even make our pain go away."

Standing up, he wobbly walked to his bedroom and opened the door when he felt his knees give up on him. His energy has been totally drained ever since his conversation with Angelica.

"What happened?!" Dereck heard a loud thud from his bedroom. He saw him sitting by the door. "Are you okay?" He helped him stand and assisted Adrian to his bed.

Adrian closed his eyes. He could feel that he would break down any minute. "Dude, can you leave me alone."

Dereck eyed him suspiciously. "Okay?" He walked to the door.

"Please close it for me. Thanks." Adrian rested his back on the soft mattress as tears started streaming down his eyes. Make all this pain go away.

Chapter 21

"**I**'ll board the plane now." Adrian gave his friend a hug.

"When are you coming back?"

"I don't know. If I have a reason to?"

Dereck tapped his shoulder. "Be careful, man. I'm gonna miss you."

"Ugh! Stop with the drama." Adrian moved his face away when Dereck tried to give him a kiss on the cheek.

Laughing, he messed up his hair. Even though Adrian was older, he was like a child most of the time so Dereck took the opportunity to act like the older brother between the two of them.

The truth was Adrian was only letting him.

"I'll go now." He fixed his eyeglasses on the bridge of his nose and then walked to the boarding gate. His step was getting heavy as he was getting close to the plane.

Adrian didn't really want to leave. However, he knew he needed to not just prove himself to Angelica's father but to his own. He realized there are so many things he couldn't have until he could achieve something greater first. What scared him was that by doing this, he might lose himself along the way.

"But I can't back out now." He blew his breath and finally boarded the plane.

Dereck was on his way home when he passed by a flower shop. "Maybe Jamaica likes flowers, should I buy her one?"

He stopped his car in front of the shop and got out of the driver's seat.

He observed the store's exterior and it was filled with plants. Going in, he opened the door and saw a masculine man arranging a set of flowers. "Welcome," said the man in a low voice.

"Hi, I want a bouquet of flowers."

"Do you have a specific flower in mind?" the flower shop owner glanced at him and he only shook his head cluelessly.

"What is she like?"

"Who?"

"The one you'll be giving the flowers to."

"Oh," Dereck paused, "She's amazing. She had been taking care of our daughter well and I wanted to thank her for that."

"Why do you like her?"

He chuckled. "Is this some sort of interview?"

"Yeah. I need it to choose the right flowers for her."

"I fell in love with her because of her eyes. It says everything and you can tell in an instant what she's feeling."

The florist stepped out of the counter and searched for the yellow lilies and yellow camellia from all the flowers inside his store. "Do you know if she has pollen allergies?"

"No, I don't."

"You can start by giving these to her." He was picking out the flowers one by one.

Dereck nodded, watching him go behind the counter again and make the bouquet he requested. He looked at the man's name written on the name tag. Andy.

"But this is not enough if your plan is to court her."

"What do you mean?"

Andy smiled. "Is this your first time courting someone?"

Dereck looked away while scratching the back of his neck. "Y-yeah."

"Just a friendly piece of advice, you should start by knowing what she likes and dislikes."

Hearing that, it came right through him. "Shit!" he muttered. I really am shameless, huh?

"Is there a problem?" Andy asked.

He just shook his head then took the bouquet Andy was handing. "Good luck."

"Thanks." Dereck left the shop uneasy. Everything was starting to sink in. How cruel he was by disregarding and avoiding Jamaica's feelings since he met her. What a jerk! He wanted to bump his head against the wall.

When he was inside his car, he placed the bouquet on the passenger's seat and thought hard about what to do next. "Jamaica might not want to see me."

Dereck took out his phone from his side pocket and dialed Angelica's number. "Hello? Angel?"

"Yes, what do you want?" She asked in an irritated voice.

"Is Jamaica there in the hospital?"

"No. She didn't come to work today. Why?"

"Nothing."

"Hey Dereck, I just want to say this. Even though you're my friend, I don't want Jamaica to end up with you. But Camila's already there and I want her to be happy. If you need help, don't hesitate to ask."

"Thanks, Angel. Uh, do you have any news about Adrian?"

"Please don't mention his name to me ever again."

"I just thought that maybe you should know. He already left for Australia and I don't have any idea if he'll come back."

"I don't care. Let him be!" Angelica abruptly ended their call.

Storming out to the emergency exit, Angelica calmed herself with a breath of fresh air. Her hand was on her waist as she fanned herself. It was so annoying! "How could he leave just like that?! Just because I told him that I wanted to end everything?"

She stayed there until she relaxed. She tried to lift her mood again and smile. When she was back in the nurses' station, there was a staff from the information desk waiting for her. "Hi, Nurse Garcia. This is for you." She handed me a bouquet of flowers that was slowly withering.

"What is this?"

"Sorry for handing it in just now. A man named Mr. Adrian Fernando came here with that when you were still on the medical mission at Tarlac."

Angelica felt her knees weaken. She was speechless.

"We're truly sorry for our incompetence." the staff bowed her head at Angelica then left.

Biting her lower lip, Angelica tried to stop herself from crying. I didn't even give him a chance to explain.

Rosette was in the dance studio training diligently after last night's play. She wanted to improve her body's condition by dancing so she had been practicing a routine for four hours already.

She was drinking water when her phone rang. "Hello?" she immediately answered.

The call was from her now-boyfriend, Stephen. "Hey, how are you?""I'm good. Are you not busy? How come you could call now?" Rosette sat on the floor and glanced up at the wall clock inside the room.

"I'm having a coffee break. Do you want to eat dinner later?"

"Sure, where are you taking me?" She lay down on the floor feeling tired. She was still catching her breath.

"Where do you want? Think of a place. By the way, why are you breathless? Are you okay?"

"Yeah, I was practicing when you called and I haven't eaten anything yet."

"What?! Why?! Tsk." She heard Stephen sigh. "Make sure you eat now before going back to practice. Please take care of yourself. I'm always worried about you."

"Hehe, I'm sorry. From now on I'll send you updates of what I'm doing."

"You don't need to do that just take care of yourself, that's enough for me."

"Okay, I'll look for something to eat now."

"Okay," he paused, "Bye."

"Bye, see you later! Love you!" Rosette said than ended the call. It was her first time saying it and she was totally embarrassed to do that. However, she didn't want to let the opportunity pass to let him know how much she appreciates him.

She stood up from lying down and she got dizzy. Rosette ignored it, carried her stuff and went out to eat.

He kept staring at his phone for a while. Stephen was baffled by what Rosette just told him. He even hasn't told it her yet. "That kid..." he muttered with a smile on his face.

He was in the rooftop garden finishing his coffee. When he was about to go back inside, Stephen noticed Angelica silently weeping in one corner. "Angel?"

Angelica looked up at him with red eyes. "Doc!"

"What happened?"

"My boyfriend left!" She cried harder. "And we didn't even get to talk properly!"

Sighing, Stephen sat beside her and patted her shoulder. "Everything happens for a reason, Angel. Maybe it was not the right time for you to reconcile. Just put your trust to God because He knows what's best for us."

Angelica wiped her tears away and asked, "Do you have a girlfriend now, Doc? I heard your conversation earlier."

Stephen kept his mouth shut not commenting. She was staring at him with wide eyes waiting for an answer. "Yeah, don't tell anyone."

"I thought you liked Jamaica?"

"That's true. I used to like her but I can see she still likes Camila's father. I don't want to be the reason the kid couldn't have a complete family."

"You're a good guy, Doc. I'm sure your girlfriend is really lucky."

"I know right?" Then the two of them laughed.

"Mommy, when is Mister coming? He did not come home last night." They were inside their room resting on the bed. The little girl was not aware that Dereck was the reason her mother was crying.

"I don't know, baby. Maybe he had some things to finish." Jamaica sadly smiled. She doesn't want to see her daughter sad. "I want to ask you a question, sweetie."

"What's your question, Mommy? Fire away!" Camila said with a laugh.

"How did you know that Mister is your daddy?"

She beamed a smile at her. "It's a secret. Don't worry, Mommy. I'm always with you. I won't leave you even if he's there."

She caressed her daughter's hair. "I know you like him. Don't worry too much about me." Jamaica smiled and gave Camila a warm embrace. She suddenly tickled her.

"Mommy!" Camila laughed out loud. She kept on squealing and crying.

Claudine knocked then opened the door. "Dear, Dereck is downstairs."

"We'll go down in a bit." Jamaica jumped out of her bed and immediately checked her face in front of the mirror. "Do I look good, baby?"

Camila gave her a thumbs up.

Breathing deeply, she calmed herself before opening the door. "Come," her daughter grabbed her outstretched hand and the two of them went downstairs.

Stepping down the stairs, she coldly looked at him. She was surprised to see him holding a bouquet of flowers but she kept a straight face.

"For you." Dereck flashed a nervous smile.

"I have allergies. Sorry, but I can't take that."

"But you like—" Jamaica covered Camila's mouth before she could reveal that her mother loves flowers.

She couldn't help but frown. Why is Mommy lying to Mister? Camila glanced at her father and saw how his shoulders fell and how his face instantly changed. He was all smiles when he came in but he was already sulking a second later.

He remembered he also bought chocolates so Dereck grabbed it from the coffee table and offered it.

Jamaica was about to reject it when Camila took it from him. "Give it to me Daddy, I'll have the chocolates. I'll give Mommy later."

Dereck smiled. "Okay, Sweetheart. Here you go." He turned to Jamaica again. "C-can we talk?"

Moving to the patio, Jamaica served their drinks before sitting on one of the seats.

"I'm sorry." Dereck said.

"About what?" She sipped on her coffee and acted like she was fine. She doesn't want to fall for him instantly and be careful from now on.

"For being a selfish jerk." He lowered his head.

"Oh, it seems like you know what you did wrong now."

Dereck raised his head and looked at her. He nodded. "Swear, I won't do it again."

"Nah, that's too early to tell. But I want to apologize too. It was my fault for not communicating well with you. If only I told you what happened..."

"It's okay, it's all in the past now." Dereck held her hand that was sitting on top of the table.

Jamaica smiled and removed her hand from his grasp. "I hope we can be good friends again."

"You gotta be joking, right?" His eyes widened in shock.

She laughed after seeing his reaction. "I'm serious. Do I look like I'm joking?" Jamaica gave him a straight face.

He cleared his throat and looked away. "No." Dereck looked again at her. "But I will still court you."

"Suit yourself. Just don't expect any answer from me." She stood up from her seat and left him alone.

Dereck suddenly played a familiar song. He grabbed her hand and turned him to her. Pressing his body against her, he held her firmly on the waist.

"W-What are you doing?" she asked.

"Nothing. I just want to have a dance with you." He removed his shoes and her slippers then led her to a dance of tango in the grass. "Do you still remember the moves?" Dereck asked, challenging her.

"Of course!" Jamaica smirked and matched his pace.

Because of the music outside, Camila got curious and peeked. She saw her parents dancing barefoot with smiles on their faces. She got envious so she ran outside.

"Daddy! Daddy! Teach me how to dance!"

Chapter 22

A black car was parked outside the Sta. Inez's residence. Inside, a man with dark gray hair and wearing a suit was watching the happy family as they played outside the front yard.

He smirked at what he witnessed before telling his driver to start the car and leave.

When the car was leaving, Stephen's car stopped and he got out holding gifts for the family.

"Daddy Stephen!" Camila ran towards him raising her arms up, asking to be carried.

Dereck was watching from the side and somewhat jealous of the closeness Stephen had with her daughter.

She knew that he was her father but Dereck could still feel an invisible wall around them that he wishes to break. But it's not easy. Forming relationships and creating bonds take a lot of time and effort.

He felt a hand on his shoulder and looked at it. When he glanced up, it was Auntie Claudine smiling at her. "Feel assured, okay? Camila grew up with Stephen. She is a smart and kind kid, she'll eventually open up to you."

Dereck smiled brightly at her, appreciating what she said.

"What is your status with Jamaica? Did she agree to be your girlfriend?" He shook his head and answered, "I'm still trying to get to know her better and I don't want to rush things this time."

"That's good, son. Know that we support you. I know my daughter well. One day, she'll be the one asking for your hand in marriage," Claudine told him followed by a hearty laugh.

He felt giddy inside but he didn't want to show it. Dereck just smiled and averted his gaze to Jamaica who was laughing with Camila in the living room.

His thoughts were interrupted when he received a phone call from an unsaved number. He already knew who it was. Moving to the kitchen, Dereck answered the call. "Why are you calling me?"

"Is that how you should be answering to your father? How ungrateful," a man with a hoarse voice said.

"Why did you call? You haven't called me even once these past few years, so why now?"

"Someone told me that you're courting a woman with a kid."

"What if I am?" Dereck replied in a low whispering voice.

"I didn't just expect you would do that. You had been angry at me for marrying a woman that was almost your age when your mother died."

"You don't know anything, Dad," he emphasized the last word before ending the call.

Just as he finished his phone call, Jamaica entered the kitchen and saw him. "Hey, what are you doing here? Why don't you join us inside?"

"Yeah, I'll do that," he paused and followed her with his gaze, "do you need anything?"

"Oh, I'll just cut some fruits to eat."

"Let me help you."

The two of them had an alone moment in the kitchen as they silently cut and peeled apples. The truth was, Jamaica was only watching him.

When it's just them, she couldn't deny the attraction that keeps pulling her to him. Like a magnet not wanting to separate from its partner.

"I'll do it," she said, placing her hand on his.

Dereck stared at their hands then looked straight into her eyes. Before, Jamaica would immediately remove her hand as if she touched a burning surface. Now, she tightened her grip on his hand and gave back the same intensity of his stares.

He slowly placed the knife and apple down on the kitchen counter to reach out to her lips for a hot and passionate kiss.

A man cleared his throat and turned out to be Joselito. "Dad..."

"Choose a private place for that, okay? The kitchen is not an appropriate area," he wiggled his eyebrows before leaving them.

Jamaica and Dereck peeked at each other, embarrassed.

He could feel her as she does. They couldn't deny the attraction they had since the start that was never really gone despite the years that passed.

"I-I'll go back inside," she said.

Dereck nodded, "I'll bring these after I finish the last one."

Jamaica just nodded without meeting his eyes again.

A few hours passed and Stephen already left when the couple invited Dereck and Jamaica to sit down and talk.

"Your mom and I have something to discuss with you, dear," Joselito started.

"What is it, Dad?"

"We talked about it and agreed to let you stay in Dereck's place."

Their daughter's eyes widened in surprise. "But-"

"We thought it would be best for Camila to always be with her father. That way they'll get closer faster."

Claudine added, "We also don't mind having another grandchild that we can take care of when both of you are busy."

"Mom!"

"We are serious dear. This is not about you and Dereck. This is all for Camila. She'll begin going to school this year right? Think about her. If she were asked about her parents, how do you think she'd answer? Do you want her classmates to hear from her that her mother and father are separated? Then she'll ask you both why it is like that. Don't wait for that to happen."

Jamaica sighed in deep thought. She raised her head and met Dereck's eyes that were staring into her.

"Are you okay?" He asked, "I mean are you okay living with me at the apartment?"

"Uh, yeah. I've already thought about it and the main reason that I went back here in the Philippines was to let Camila know you and be close to you. I think this is the best opportunity."

Dereck nodded in understanding. They were on the balcony watching the busy afternoon street across them. "It's good then. I don't want to pressure you or anything like that but I'll take it as a chance to show to both of you that I've changed and I want to make everything right." He gently held her hands.

Jamaica was surprised by his warm hand. Before, she always felt worried and scared when Dereck touches him because she knew that what we were doing was wrong. Now, that simple gesture was perfect. It was what she needed. Assurance.

She had been waiting for him to decide for himself and stand firmly his ground on whatever decision he makes.

Smiling back at him, Jamaica squeezed his hand.

Because Adrian was not in the apartment, Dereck was living alone for quite some time. He brought Jamaica and Camila over as he carried their baggage.

"Welcome to our apartment," he said with a smile on his face. "I'll guide you to my room. You can use that. I'll use Adrian's room." They passed by the living room and kitchen to the rooms they'll use. Dereck opened the door on his right widely. "Here's my room."

"Wow!" Camila exclaimed. She saw that the bed was filled with stuffed toys that she could play with. She ran to it and jumped to get one toy.

What Jamaica noticed was the design of the whole room. The bed sheets, the curtains, and the walls. "Did you arrange the room for us?" She didn't hear any response from Dereck so she looked at him and saw he was covering his mouth with his hand but she could clearly see how red his ears were. He's embarrassed!

She looked away and commented, "The room is very beautiful. Thank you."

Dereck only smiled. "I'll leave you now so you can relax and take a rest while I prepare our food. What do you want to eat?"

"Camila's not really picky about her food. She's allergic to seafood."

"Yup, yup. I don't like shrimp!"

"Really?" Dereck asked.

"Yeah. Why?"

"I'm also allergic to seafood."

"Maybe she got that from you," Jamaica gave him a faint smile. He only smiled back before closing the door as he left the room.

Jamaica sat down on the bed, contemplating if she did the right thing. She looked at her daughter who was happily playing. "Do you like it here, baby?"

"Yes! I will always be with Daddy."

"Daddy? You're calling Mister Daddy?"

Little Camila nodded. "He's my Daddy. I just like teasing him, that's why I call him Mister."

"Oh you, naughty girl," Jamaica pinched her daughter's cheek lightly which made both of them laugh. "It's good that you like it here. You will go to school this year. Are you excited?"

"Yes!" The girl jumped on her mom. Her laughs grew louder. They begin tickling each other; they didn't notice Dereck standing in the doorway watching them.

"Looks like both of you are having fun, huh?"

The girls stopped and looked at him before smiling wickedly just to include him in their game. "Uh-oh," Dereck ran to the living room away from them.

"Daddy, why are you running away!" Camilla yelled running with her small legs.

He stopped in his tracks upon hearing her call him. Dereck didn't know what to feel to finally hear his daughter call him 'daddy'. I thought I wouldn't get to hear her say it.

'Gotcha!" Camila caught up to him and held his legs. "Why are you running away, Daddy? You don't want us to tickle you?"

He looked down at her and the shock was still visible on his face. Slowly a smile crept on his face as he sat down to level his face on her. "Gotcha!" His hands were already around her small figure and tickled Camila on her waist.

She laughed brightly and it warmed his heart. He wanted to cherish every moment with her. With them.

Dereck whispered something in Camila's ear, "Let's go to mommy and tickle her instead." The little girl nodded in enthusiasm then he carried her just to run after Jamaica.

"Why are you running after me!" She breathlessly screamed and circled around the couch to get away from them.

The room was filled with laughter and giggles. The three of them lay down on the floor exhausted. "Let's just order chicken and pizza," Dereck told them.

"Yeah, but after taking a nap," replied Jamaica.

"Okay, what flavors do you want? I'll order now and schedule the delivery," he asked. When no one was answering he pinned his elbow to check on Jamaica only to find out she was already asleep. Camila was between them looking at him.

"Mister, I am not giving you permission yet to marry Mommy, okay?"

"I thought you were already calling me daddy?"

Camila turned towards him. "Yes..." She snuggled closer to him for a hug and closed her eyes, yawning.

Dereck turned to face them and closed his eyes to sleep.

He woke up hearing little noises in the kitchen. "Shhh... Sweetheart, you'll wake Daddy," it was Jamaica's voice.

"Sorry, Mommy. What are you cooking?"

Dereck's eyebrows knitted in curiosity. Cooking? Did they go out shopping? He slowly moved without making any noise and peeked at the kitchen. Jamaica was occupied cooking their dinner while Camila was sitting in one of the seats while playing with her toy.

He stood up and sneaked behind his daughter and tapped her shoulder. The little girl looked behind and gasped. Dereck placed a finger between his lips.

Camila immediately understood and nodded her head. She quietly giggled feeling giddy as she watched her father trying to get closer to her mommy.

Closer, Dereck stepped near Jamaica and swiftly slid his hands around her waist for a hug. She startled moving her head, bumping his nose. "Ouch!"

Jamaica cried in pain while caressing the back of her head. Upon turning around, she discovered Dereck with a bleeding nose. "Oh my," she panicked looking for the tissue paper.

"I'll be fine," He took the tissue from her hand. "I'll just wash it in the bathroom," Dereck left the kitchen.

Jamaica sighed then heard their daughter giggling. "Sweetheart, was it funny?" Camila smiled widely and nodded. She followed Dereck to see if he was really alright.

"Dereck?"

He was washing his nose but the bleeding won't stop so she stopped what he was doing. "Stand straight and look up." Dereck obeyed her since she was the doctor. Jamaica grabbed a towel and watered it a little before wiping his nose.

She touched her face as she tried removing all the blood. "Aren't you feeling dizzy?"

Dereck lightly shook his head. He watched her and he could see how worried she was. Grabbing her hand, Jamaica stopped. "I'm fine now."

Putting her hand down, she tightened her grasp on his hand. Dereck was observing her as she bit her lower lip.

"Let's eat," He said with a smile.

Chapter 23

The next day, Dereck was up early since he needs to teach at the dance school. He was eating breakfast the moment Jamaica came out of the room. "Good morning," she greeted.

Dereck couldn't look at her because she was wearing a huge shirt and shorts that were revealing her white skin. He gulped his food down hardly since it was his first time seeing her in that kind of nightwear. He looked away drinking his coffee instead.

Jamaica tilted her head in confusion. Why isn't he answering me? Is there a problem? She headed straight to the cupboard to get a glass and fetch water before eating anything.

"Do you want to go to the dance school with me? Let's bring Camila along," he offered without looking at her.

"But she's still asleep," she told him.

"Mommy... Daddy..." Camila got out of their room in her pink pajamas.

"Good morning, baby. Do you want to go to daddy's school?" Jamaica asked but the little girl just stared at them.

They arrived at the school welcomed by one of the staff on the front desk. "Good morning, Sir, Ma'am."

"Good morning," greeted Dereck, "let's go to my office," he led Jamaica and Camila to a tiny room at the end of the hall.

Inside was a wooden table, a sofa set, and a mini coffee table at the center while two cabinets were at one corner near his table. Behind his table was the glass window over-looking the busy streets of the barangay.

"Take a seat first. I'll just look for something," Dereck opened the cabinets and started rummaging inside. "Found it!"

He pulled out an old tutu that could fit Camila. It was pinkish white and also has ballet shoes. "Do you want to learn ballet, sweetheart?"

Camila doesn't have any idea what ballet was so he brought her inside the ballet classroom. There, the little girl saw girls her age wearing the same tutu dress Dereck was holding and ballet shoes. Their hair was pulled back neatly and nicely into a bun.

The teacher called the students to come into the center to start their warm-up and that was when Camila noticed the only boy in class. She couldn't take her eyes off him.

The little boy was inches taller than her, had the same black eyes and hair as hers and, had similar pale white skin. But what captured her attention was his beautiful smile.

So, Camilla tugged Jamaica's shirt and whispered, "I want too."

Her mother gasped, "You want to learn ballet?"

Camila nodded in excitement. Dereck, on the other hand, gave Jamaica the uniform.

She got dressed all ready for learning a new skill. However, instead of adding her to the group where the cute boy was, she was in the corner sitting on the floor to learn the proper stretching for beginners.

She wanted to cry. That's not what she signed up for!

Jamaica felt a hand on her hand and looked beside her only to see Dereck reflecting how her smile was beautifully worn on her face. "Let's go," he whispered.

"But—"

He pulled her upstairs to an empty classroom. "What are we doing here?"

Dereck played a familiar song. It was her favorite song!

"May I have this dance?"

Smiling, Jamaica accepted his offered hand and he pulled her into an embrace. The two of them swayed on the dance-floor enjoying the moment of being together.

The first time they danced in the song was when he teaches her how to dance for the wedding party of Dereck's father. Then, they danced to it again when Jamaica attended the dance class. And now.

Just their hands brushing, sends butterflies to their stomachs. Dereck bored directly into Jamaica as if it were just the two of them. He tightened his grip around her waist not wanting to let go of her.

I'm melting because of his gaze, Jamaica thought but she couldn't look away. She could see his face was leaning closer into a

kiss. She panicked. Wait, I'm not ready!

Before she could even pull back, his soft lips were already on hers kissing her senselessly as if his life depended on it.

Her knees got weaker and had to hold onto his arms for support, still, it wasn't enough and Dereck felt that so he steadied her and lifted her up on top of the cabinet near the window.

Out of breath, Dereck pulled away resting his forehead on hers. He still couldn't believe what they had shared.

This time there were no confusions, there were no uncertainties, and there were no hesitations about their relationships.

Actions were enough to convey what they truly felt for each other.

He smiled. She smiled back. A sudden burst of laughter escaped their lips thinking of how silly they might have been.

"Gosh, I love your laughs," Dereck confessed to her.

"Oh, really?" Jamaica knitted her eyebrows then raised the right one.

Dereck admittingly nodded, his smile never leaving his face. He pinched her nose lightly. He was about to kiss her again but she immediately covered her mouth. He frowned and Jamaica pointed towards the door. There, Rosette and Stephen were standing by the doorway.

"Uh, Direk, we didn't see anything but it's time to get out of this room. I need to use it."

Dereck lowered his head pouting like a little kid so Jamaica leaned to his ear and whispered, "We can continue it later, if you like." His face lightened up which caused her to laugh again. She pinched his cheeks hard. "Ouch!"

"You're cute!" Jamaica jumped down the cabinet. "You can use the room now, Rose." She smiled at Rosette and Stephen before exiting. Dereck followed her in a heartbeat. He was about to step out of the door when he came back and asked, "Are you two dating?"

Jamaica pulled her out. "Come on, leave them be." He looked at her. "Do you know something?" She just smiled.

When they visited the ballet classroom, the lesson was just about to end. Jamaica was surprised to see their daughter so happy. The teacher walked towards them with Camila and said, "She really is flexible for her age. You better enroll her and have continuous lessons while she's young."

"Do you want that, sweetheart?" Jamaica asked Camila. She just nodded smiling from ear to ear.

All of a sudden, an emergency team entered the premises hurrying to the second floor. Jamaica followed upstairs because of the commotion. She ran to Stephen and asked what happened.

"She just had an episode. I already did the first aid."

"I'll check her bag for her medications," she offered. Jamaica looked around and saw a gray tote bag in one corner. She immediately opened it but saw nothing. There were no medicines, only clothes. "There's no meds here, Stephen."

Rosette was carried in a stretcher to the ambulance and Stephen carried her things before riding as well. "Where will you take her?" He asked one of the responders."Stephen Brown Hospital. It is the nearest hospital from here."

"Okay. Thank you."

Arriving at the hospital, Rosette was brought to the emergency room and was aided by the nurses. Stephen headed to the pharmacy and asked one of the staff their, "Hi, I would just like to ask about Rosette Morales' last purchase of her medicine?"

The staff looked into the computer for the records and told him, "According to the data here Sir, the last purchase was three months ago."

"Three months ago?" His eyebrows knitted in confusion. "Alright, thank you." He went back to the emergency room and waited for Rosette to wake up. Stephen sat on one of the stools and crossed his arms over his chest.

He received a call from one of the residents asking for advice so he stepped out for a while and when he came back to her side, she was already awake feeling weak. "Care to explain what happened, missy?"

Rosette laughed nervously. She knew he was already angry seeing how his jaws clenched. Her shoulders fell and sighed. "I'm getting tired of taking my medications. I think I'm not getting well even if I diligently drink my maintenance."

"But you still want to get well?"

"Of course!" Rosette yelled, "I can't do a lot of things because of this."

"Then you shouldn't stop taking it."

"What if I have this condition forever?"

Ahh... that's what she's worried about. Stephen smiled and said, "Don't worry 'cause I'll be taking care of you."

She looked at him shocked, "Is that a proposal?"

"Think how you'd like it to be. Just know this," he leaned closer and looked directly into her eyes, "I'll be your personal doctor and nurse."

Rosette engulfed him in a hug surprising him. "Thank you!"

He cleared his throat and hid the forming blush on his cheeks.

Angelica's phone was ringing for the nth time but she'd rather work than answer it. Another nurse tapped her shoulder and asked, "Aren't you gonna answer it?" she peeked, "it's you, dad."

"I don't need to. He'll probably tell me the next schedule of my blind date."

"Wow! At least you have a blind date unlike most of us here. We're stuck with work and we don't have time to date."

She just laughed at the remark of her colleague. Deep inside she'd rather work than meet men. She doesn't have any energy left to get to know someone else after experiencing the pain of liking someone who likes you back but doesn't have the courage to fight for it.

I don't want to go through that all over again.

Angelica's thoughts were interrupted by a knock on the counter of the nurses' station. "Busy?"

"Stephen! Aren't you on leave right now?"

"Yeah, but I had to come 'cause Rosette was sent by an ambulance earlier."

"Oh no, what happened?" Angelica abruptly stood up.

"She stopped drinking her maintenance for three months."

"Why? She's getting tired?"

"Yeah, looks like it. You know kids think differently than adults."

"So, why did you come here? Is there anything I can do?"

"Can you befriend her and teach her what are the other things she could do besides drinking her meds to help her get well?"

"Hmm... I can do that. I guess that's better than attending those blind dates that my father had been set up for me," she said with a laugh.

"Why? Don't you want to attend those?" Angelica went silent. Stephen nodded in understanding, "Don't pressure yourself. Time will heal every wound," he tapped her shoulder before going back to the emergency room.

At home, Camila was already sleeping soundly while Jamaica and Dereck decided to have coffee before going to bed. "It looks like she's too tired," Jamaica commented chuckling. She took a sip of her coffee and got her tongue burned.

"Are you okay?" Dereck stood next to her.

"I'm fine. It's not that serious."

He sat back on his chair in front of her then asked, "Oh, what would we do when Camila starts school? Uh, should she have my surname by now?"

"That's easy. I'll just file a request to update her name," she answered before having another sip.

Dereck nodded sadly then drank his coffee to hide the disappointment on his face. He thought she would open up about their marriage to legalize their relationship. His phone vibrated so he checked what it was and saw a text message from his father.

From: DadI want to meet the woman you've been seeing and her daughter. If you don't introduce them to me, I'll find a way to see them.

Dereck stood up from his seat surprised and worried about his father's threat. "Why is there a problem?" Jamaica asked, "You look pale."

"I think I'm just sleepy. I'll go to bed now," he smiled then walked past her. She looked at him with concern as she watched him go to his bedroom.

He sat on his bed and texted a reply to his father.

To: Dad

Don't you dare see them. I'll introduce them when the right time comes.

Upon sending the message, he rested his back and stared at the ceiling. I need to do something before Dad interferes. He closed his eyes and let the fatigue take him over.

Chapter 24

Jamaica was passing by the hospital's lobby when a group of nurses and doctors were rushing a patient to the emergency room.

She glanced at the patient and recognized who it was. Mr. Sy! Her eyes widened in surprise so she ran behind them. "What happened?"

"The old man fainted because of hypertension."

A nurse came up to them and said, "He's a VIP here in the hospital. His name is Fredrick Sy."

She wanted to stay until Mr. Sy woke up but she had been receiving messages from her fellow residents and from Stephen. I'll just visit him later.

Dereck received a phone call while he was cooking breakfast. He exasperatedly sigh thinking it was his father again but to his surprise it was Jamaica. "Hello?"

"Dereck..."

"Yes?" He smiled.

"It's about your dad... He's confined here right now. It was discovered that he has heart failure. I think you should come and visit him."

His expression changed. He tightly gripped the phone in his hand. Dereck never imagined his father could get weak and helpless. He remembered him during his childhood days as someone vigorous.

"I'll be there."

"Okay, I'll check up on him when I'm not busy. Take your time preparing and just bring Camila."

"Okay."

"I'll be going now."

"Jamaica..."

"Hmm..."

"Thank you."

"Just let me know when you're here."

"Bye."

"Bye."

Dereck placed his phone down back on top of the kitchen counter then finished what he was cooking.

"Mister, I'm hungry," Camila was wiping her eyes as she stepped into the kitchen.

"I cooked eggs and bacon. Let's eat now."

She climbed up the chair and sat waiting for Dereck to serve the food.

He placed a plate with rice, egg, and bacon in front of her and in front of him before he sat down. "Uh, baby..."

Camila looked up at him.

"Do you want to meet your other grandpa?" He asked nervously.

"Other grandpa? What do you mean another grandpa?" She furrowed her eyebrows and tilted her head.

"Yes, it's my daddy. Do you want to meet him?"

Her eyes widened, "Your daddy?" She nodded excitedly.

After visiting all patients for the morning rounds, Jamaica went straight to the VIP room where Mr. Sy was confined. She quietly opened the door and walked up to the bed.

Mr. Sy was still asleep. He was still how she remembered him but with grayish-white hair and visible lines of old age.

She held his hand and just stared at him. Minutes later, the old man slowly opened his eyes. "Mr. Sy, how are you feeling?"

Jamaica noticed he wanted to sit up so she helped him raise the bed a little. "I'll call your doctor." She hurriedly ran outside to inform the desk then came back to talk to him a bit. Grabbing the stool, she sat down. "I would like to introduce myself. I am Jamaica Claire Sta. Inez, Dereck's friend."

"I know you," Mr. Sy was looking at her with recognition. "You're the one he brought to my wedding party."

"Yes," Jamaica nervously let out a chuckle.

"And I know that you have a daughter and he is seeing you."

"Oh,"

"Look Miss, sorry to burst your bubble but I don't want my son to get involved with someone who already has a child."

"Mr. Sy, the truth is my daughter is—" The doctors and nurses assigned to Mr. Sy came in that Jamaica didn't have a chance to tell him everything. She quietly stepped out of the room and went back to work.

Dereck entered the hospital's lobby while holding Camila's hand. They stopped in a corner to call Jamaica. It was only ringing and his call couldn't get through. "I think Mommy is busy." He held Camila's hand again and headed to the information table to ask.

"Good morning, Sir. How may I help you?"

"Hi, I just want to ask where can I find a patient named Fredrick Sy?"

The receptionist searched for the name and told him, "The patient is at the VIP wing in the seventh floor.""Okay, thank you." Dereck carried Camila since it was a long walk to the elevator. He held her on one arm while his other hand was holding a basket of fruits he bought for his father.

Camila placed her hands on his shoulder and asked, "Mister, does he look like you?"

He impassively looked at her. "You're calling me Mister again."

She just giggled, enjoying his expressionless expressions.

"I think we look alike but he's older now." He stepped in the elevator car and pushed number seven.

At the seventh floor Dereck got out of the car and walked up to a nurse, "Hi, I'm here to visit a patient named Fredrick Sy, where is his room?"

"What is your relation to the patient, sir?" the nurse asked.

"I'm his son."

"Oh, okay, he's in the first room on the right."

"Thank you."

Dereck put Camila down then opened the door. His father immediately saw him even just at the doorway. He saw his expression change while looking at the kid.

"I see you brought that woman's daughter here."

"What do you mean? Have you already met Jamaica?" Dereck got worked up.

Camila was staring at the old man. "Mister, he really looks just like you!"

Both men glanced at her. She suddenly tried to climb the bed so Dereck helped her.

"Hello grandpa! My name is Camila. I am Mister and Mommy's daughter."

Fredrick furrowed his eyebrows. "What does she mean by that?"

Dereck scratched the back of his head and replied, "Truth is, she's my daughter with Jamaica."

"How did that happen?"

"At your wedding. Something happened between the two of us but I just knew recently."

"If that's the case, when do you plan to get married?"

"Mister can't marry Mommy," Camila butted in the conversation.

"And why is that?" Fredrick smiled asking.

"Because I don't want to share my Mommy."

The elder laughed loudly. "I think you have a possessive daughter right here."

"Why do you need to marry? You are my daddy even if you and Mommy are not married, right?"

"But you only know that. Other people don't know that he is your daddy. What if pretty girls like your mommy take him away?"

Camila's eyes began to water and wailed.

Dereck panicked because she rarely cries. "Baby," he carried her and caressed her back, "don't cry. I won't leave."

Fredrick was just watching his son with a smile on his face. He was enjoying the very scene in front of his eyes.

Jamaica entered the room and was surprised to see Dereck and Camila.

"Mommy!" Camila reached out her arms to her so Dereck passed their daughter to her.

"What's happening?"

"My dad is teasing her."

Fredrick spoke and said, "I am asking when the two of you will get married?"

Jamaica gave Dereck a glance. She was just waiting for what he would do next.

"We'll leave now and wait for you at home," Dereck said. He was carrying Camila since she's sleeping on his shoulder.

"Okay," Jamaica smiled. "Drive safe."

He nodded but he didn't move a step. He wanted to give her a kiss even just on the cheek, however, he was not sure what was on her mind and if it was alright to do so.

"I- uh... we'll get going."

Jamaica finished her shift and was already walking out of the hospital when Angelica hooked her arm on her shoulder. "Hey, you're already going home?"

"Yeah, I want to talk to Dereck about what his father said."

"What is it?"

"He was asking when we'll get married."

"Ooohhh..." Angelica's smile widened. "But before you do that, don't you want to go out with me first? Let's go to Rowena's and visit Rosette."

"Huh?"

"Let's have a girls' night out?"

Rosette was rehearsing her contemporary dance performance for one of her classes. Her mind was filled with worries because of her condition. Even if Stephen told her that he is always by her side, still, she doesn't want to be a burden to him. To her mother. To anybody else.

Her phone was ringing and vibrating but she was not even checking it.

She continued to dance and her movements got bigger with more force as if she was fighting in the air. Her heart was getting heavier, she couldn't contain it anymore.

She broke down and cried.

When she was already calm and composed, Rosette grabbed her phone to see who called and texted.

Some were from Stephen, some were from Angelica, and a text message from Jamaica.

She opened the message and read.

From: Jamaica

Hey Rose, let's meet up at your mom's resto and have a chat! See you there at 7.

Rosette wiped her tears away and typed a reply.

To: Jamaica

I'll be there. See you! :)

She immediately stood up, gathered her things and ran out of the dance room.

The girls were gathered in a table drinking sodas and munching fries for their appetizer.

"Why did you suddenly want to meet up?" Rosette asked Angelica and Jamaica.

"I wanna hear some gossip from Jamaica here and we want to include you in our bondings from now on," Angelica told her. "So," she looked at Jamaica, "what's the marriage thing about?"

Jamaica was eating the fries continuously then heaved a sigh. "Dereck's father, the VIP patient brought earlier, was asking for a marriage date. Dereck isn't even doing anything ever since I told him that I want to take things slow."

The waiter came to their table and served the burgers they ordered were served.

"Seriously, girl, why are you going back and forth? What do you really want to do?" Angelica asked. "What do you want to happen? Isn't it that you went home here to settle things with him?"

Jamaica nodded.

"You should let him see that," Rosette told her. "Direk might want to do something but he's unsure 'cause he doesn't know what you think or what you feel. Let him know."

"The result may not be what you hoped for but at least you tried," added Angelica.

"I'll do that."

"Make sure you're doing it because you want it and you're ready for it, okay? Not because his father's pressuring you." Angelica said. "You know, I'm good at giving advice to others' relationships but I don't know how to handle mine." She chugged down the soda she was drinking.

"Do you have any news about him?" Rosette carefully asked.

"No, I don't. And I like it better that I have no idea what he's been up to."

"Why?" Jamaica inquired before taking another huge bite on her burger.

"My heart's at peace this way."

The two girls nodded in understanding and did not ask anymore. They knew what she meant.

Angelica and Jamaica then lifted their gazes to Rosette. She lifted her eyebrows and told them, "I don't wanna tell you about mine tonight. Maybe some other time."

Jamaica arrived home around eleven in the evening already feeling tired. She didn't notice Dereck was sitting on the couch waiting for her. "Why are you so late?"

"Huh?" She raised her head and saw him. "Oh, I had dinner with Angelica and Rosette."

She placed her bag down and walked straight to the living room where he is. She then sat beside her.

"What did the three of you talk about?" He glanced at her.

"A lot of things" Jamaica yawned while stretching her arms up.

Dereck was watching her every move. How she closes and opens her eyes, how she sighs and pouts her lips after. Whatever she does, his eyes never go away.

Suddenly, she turned her head and met his warm gaze.

No one spoke. But it was fine.

Jamaica bit her lower lip and avoided his gaze. It was so warm she felt like she was melting already.

She remembered what the girls told her to let him know what she truly feels. And what she did next relayed that to Dereck fully and completely.

She turned her body and leaned in closer to him, closing the gap between them and sealing his lips with a kiss.

Chapter 25

The kiss was not like the ones they had shared. Jamaica was straddling on top of him kissing him passionately.

It was happening so fast that Dereck was too overwhelmed and tried to catch up with her. He started to feel excited about what was about to happen when she suddenly stopped. Her head lightly fell on his shoulder. Unconscious.

Shocked, Dereck shook her a little but still, Jamaica was dead asleep snoring soundly. He chuckled, shaking his head in disbelief. "What will I do about you? Huh?" He whispered even though he knew she wouldn't hear. They stayed like that for a few minutes and he slowly closed his eyes.

Jamaica woke up feeling tingly feathery kisses all over her face. She turned her face away but the kisses didn't stop. Instead, it went on her neck up to her shoulder blades.

Huh? I thought Camila's kissing me.

She slowly opened her eyes and noticed that she was not in the room she was using with Camila. Her gaze went to Dereck on top of her. "What are you doing?" She hissed.

"Waking you up?"

"Well, I'm awake now so get off me."

Camila unexpectedly opened the door and caught them at that position. "Mister," she just glanced at the two, "I'm hungry," then turned her back from them.

Jamaica was surprised that their daughter didn't react because Camila used to be upset when Dereck acted sweet to her.

Dereck was about to kiss Jamaica and this time on the lips but Camila entered again. "Mister, is my baby brother coming?"

"Not yet, baby. Why?"

"I want to have a playmate."

Jamaica couldn't believe what she was hearing. When did the two of them have this kind of conversation? What is Dereck teaching our daughter? She pinched him on the side of his waist that made him yelp in pain.

"Ouch!" Dereck glanced at her, frowning.

She pushed him away, got out of bed, and stepped outside. "Sweetheart, let's have breakfast!"

Dereck smirked remembering the conversation he had with Camila.

They were already at home and he was playing dolls with her so he asked, "Baby, don't you want to have a playmate?"

Camila's eyes sparkled with interest and excitedly bobbed her head. "I want!"

"But we can only make a baby brother or sister for you if we get married," he pouted as if he was really sad.

"I give you my permission, Mister! You can marry Mommy." Camila smiled widely.

Dereck opened his palm in the air, "Appear!" Camila tapped his hand with full force.

His strides were getting larger as he try to catch the last bus to work. Adrian was almost running, breathless when he heard someone call "Angelica!"

He stopped in his tracks. His heart skipped a beat and hoped it was her. So Adrian slowly turned his head and looked behind where the voice came from. Sadly, it was a different person. He already knew that still he really wished for a miracle.

Chuckling, he shook his head and ran to catch the bus that stopped in the stop area.

Angelica just arrived at the hospital when she bumped into Dereck. "Hey!"

"Hey," he smiled at her.

"Are you here to visit your dad?" She remembered what Jamaica told her the other night.

"Yeah, I wanted to talk to him about something."

Angelica squinted her eyes, "Hmmm...I can sense it's about you and Jamaica. Are we invited to the wedding?"

He blushed, looking away. Dereck cleared his throat and changed the subject. "Adrian told me he'll come back next month. Are you going to see him?"

She felt a pang in her chest. Hearing his name made her uncomfortable, but she stayed calm and said, "I don't know. Let's see if an opportunity will come for us to meet. I'll leave it all to fate."

He gave her a reassuring smile and tapped her on the shoulder.

Dereck opened the door and slightly bowed his head to greet his father. "Why are you here again? Did you miss me that much?"

"Well, not really. I'm here to ask for help."

Fredrick maintained a poker face and said, "Let's hear it first."

Getting out of his car, Stephen stared at the building and nervously let out his breath. "I can do this!"

He stepped into the restaurant and was immediately greeted by Rowena. "Doc Stephen! It's nice to see you! Are you here to visit Rosette?"

Rowena doesn't have any idea that he likes her daughter.

"Actually ma'am, I'm here to talk to you," he flashed his sweet smile.

"Why? Is there something wrong with Rosette?" The mother panicked.

"No ma'am, it's not about that." He led her to sit on a chair then he sat across from her. "I want to ask for your permission to court her."

"Huh? Aren't you in a relationship already?"

Stephen was surprised. "I, uh—I haven't courted her properly."

"Oh, if that's the case it is alright with me if you court her. I know my daughter." She said with a laugh, "she's so obvious, you know, that she likes you. I notice how fast her expression changes when you're the one she's texting."

He blushed, embarrassed. "Sorry for asking permission a little late."

"No problem. And I like you, Doc." Rowena placed her hand on top of his and tapped it lightly. "Take care of my daughter."

"I will."

A few days passed and Fredrick was already out of the hospital. He took out his phone and dialed Jamaica's number.

"Hello?"

"It's me, Ms. Sta. Inez, Mr. Sy."

"Ah yes, how may I help you?"

"I'd like to meet you. Are you available later this evening? I'll send the address."

"Yes, sir. I'll be there."

"See you later," he ended the call with a smile on his face.

Jamaica was surprised by Mr. Sy's call. Why did he suddenly call? She was already fixing herself before going out of the hospital.

She arrived at the restaurant feeling nervous so she bit her lower lip before taking a step inside. She spotted Mr. Sy's table so she walked toward him.

"Hi, Mr. Sy," she bowed her head a little.

"Have a seat, dear."

Jamaica sat down across from him.

"Have you eaten dinner? Let's eat first." My. Sy called the waiter and they ordered their meals.

While waiting, Mr. Sy asked her. "So, how are you?"

Jamaica was startled. "I—I'm fine. I'm busy with work at the hospital right now."

Mr. Sy nodded. "Dereck told me that your daughter is his."

"Yes, I raised her in the US and I just told Dereck the truth." She was really nervous 'cause she felt like she was being interrogated all of a sudden.

Even though he did not say anything afterward she explained her side of the story.

"I got scared that time when I discovered that I was pregnant. I didn't know what Dereck truly feels about me."

The food came so they began eating first.

"How about now?"

Jamaica raised her head. "Now?"

"How about now? Do you know what he feels about you?"

She just nodded her head.

"What are you feeling about him now? Do you still feel the same?"

She looked down avoiding his gaze. Jamaica's feelings for Dereck never changed no matter how long they had been apart.

When she met the old man's gaze he was smiling as if he already knew her answer.

"Can you give me your best available time for the wedding day?"

Jamaica couldn't believe what she just heard.

"You heard me. I'll take care of your wedding. Just give me a date you prefer."

Is this for real? She thought. Is it finally happening?

Two weeks later, Jamaica was handing out wedding invitations to her colleagues at the hospital.

Everyone was surprised she was getting married to Stephen because they thought that the two of them were the hospital's couple.

She just laughed at their unbelievable presumptions about her relationship. "Doc Stephen has a girlfriend."

The other doctors in the room looked at each other with wide eyes and smiling faces. "I know you're curious who that girlfriend is," Jamaica chuckled, "you can ask him."

Dereck was in front of the mirror inside the bathroom wearing a towel below his waist and shaving his beard. He wanted to look clean since he decided to pick up Jamaica at the hospital. She was in the night shift and will be getting out in two hours. He already finished bathing and dressing up Camila so he won't hurry too much.

After shaving, he went inside his room to dry his hair, change his clothes, and checked if he was dressed well enough.

"Baby, do I look good?" he came out of his room asking Camila who was playing on the living room.

"Mister? Where is your beard?"

"I removed it. Am I more handsome now?"

The kid nodded enthusiastically.

"Alright. Let's go pick Mommy then we'll eat something nice."

They arrived at the hospital after an hour and a half drive. Dereck noticed a lot of people glancing his way as he and Camila walked toward the information desk. "Hi Sir, how may I help you?"

"May I know where can I find Doctor Jamaica Claire Sta. Inez?"

"In the Pedia Department? That's on the third floor, sir."

"Thank you." Dereck then carried Camila into his arms and went to ride the elevator.

In the third floor, he stepped out of the car and immediately searched for the nurses' station.

"Hi, Miss, where can we find Doc Jamaica?"

"Oh," the nurse got surprised upon seeing him. Just like what was the reaction of the others ever since he entered the building. "What is your business with Doc Jamaica, sir?"

"We're here to—"

"What are the two of you doing here?" Jamaica called Dereck and Camila's attention when she saw them standing at the nurses' station

"Mommy!" He put Camila down then she ran towards her.

Jamaica carried her repeating her question. "What are you doing here?" She walked up to Dereck with a smile on her face.

"We thought it'll be good to have dinner outside so we picked you up."

A nurse interrupted their conversation just to ask her, "Doc, is he your boyfriend?"She nodded then introduced Camila, "This is our daughter."

"Hi little girl, what's your name?"

"I'm Daphne Camila Sta. Inez. I'm seven years old."

The nurse then commented, "You'll get your daddy's surname once they get married, huh?"

Jamaica just smiled thinking that everything is going well already. She just wished that before they get married Dereck would propose to him so she glanced at him who was only listening to the nurse talking. "Come on now. I was about to go out when you came."

They said goodbye to the nurse and headed out of the hospital.

Dereck brought Jamaica and Camila to a fancy restaurant.

"Wow!" Jamaica exclaimed, "how come you brought us here? Is there any special occasion?"

"Nothing. I just wanted to have a nice dinner with the two of you."

They were guided by a waiter to a seat for three. "This way, Sir, Ma'am."

As they sat down, the waiter handed them the menu before leaving them.

Dereck was sitting across from Jamaica and Camila so he quietly tapped the engagement ring box in his pocket. "Are you ready to order?" He then called the waiter.

"Yes, Sir?" the waiter came up holding a notepad and pen in his hands.

"We'd like to have lamb chops, a burger, Greek salad, Sun-dried Tomato Herb pasta, three drinks of lemonade, and a blueberry cheesecake.

After repeating the order, the waiter went away to process it.

Dereck could see Jamaica was observing the place. She was like that. Quietly looking around, from the ceilings to the walls up to the floors. Appreciating everything there is and enjoying every moment she could have.

Jamaica already had an idea the moment Dereck brought them to the restaurant. She wasn't expecting anything really but something tells her that he'll do something unexpected.

She suddenly heard Dereck exasperated sigh so she looked at him surprised. "Is there a problem?"

He wet his lips then bit them and did it a couple of times. She could see he was shaking. He let out his breath nervously.

She didn't want to see him unconscious because of anxiety so she said, "Are you proposing to me right now?"

Dereck looked up at her, shocked. His mouth was wide open, "What—How—" He slowly placed his hand on the table that was holding the box.

Jamaica held his hand and smiled. "It's a yes. You don't have to say anything more because I can already feel it every time."

He stood up from his seat, walked to where she was sitting and pulled her up for a hug. "You don't know how happy I am. I already know we're getting married but to hear the confirmation from you, I can't say anything more," Dereck hugged her tightly and she could melt inside his arms.

"I'll have a baby brother now, right?" Camila butted in.

"Don't worry baby, Mommy and I will work on that."

"Hey!" Jamaica lightly slapped him on the back.

Epilogue

"You may now kiss your bride," the officiant told Dereck after saying their vows.

He couldn't wait for the officiant to finish, he immediately held her face and sealed her lips with a kiss. Then, Dereck stared straight into her loving eyes.

Family and friends applauded for the delightful yet touching moment. Among the guests were Stephen, Rosette, and Angelica, a few of Dereck's actors, and Jamaica's invited colleagues in the Pediatric department.

Their wedding was held in the hotel and so was the party. The room was designed with a mini stage one end with a red carpet. Then the round tables were placed around it where the guests were seated.

While everyone was waiting, the quartet was playing love songs. The emcee took over for the program while Dereck and Jamaica were given time to change into more comfortable attire.

Jamaica was with Angelica and Rosette to help her while Dereck was with Stephen. They have their own rooms that they used before the wedding and they were about to go there but Dereck couldn't wait to be with Jamaica.

He grabbed her arm and told the others, "Can't I have a break with my wife?"

Angelica rolled her eyes at him, "Uh, no you can't because there's still a program. Do that later when we're finished."

Stephen pulled Dereck to his room.

Later on, they were called again by the emcee and were welcomed by the guests as a new husband and wife.

The music began playing then the host announced, "Let's give it up for Mr. and Mrs. Sy!"

Dereck and Jamaica stood at the center of the room facing each other, and swayed along to the music.

The band was playing the theme song from the movie Enchanted, So Close. Their theme song.

Jamaica chuckled, shaking her head, "You never change. This is not my favorite song, you know."

"I know. It's mine." Dereck wiggled his eyebrows while his hands tightened around her waist.

While everyone was busy watching the couple, someone entered the ballroom quietly. He stayed by the door looking for the person he was looking for. Slowly, he walked up to the table where she was sitting and lightly tapped her on the shoulder.

She turned her head looking up, "A-Adrian?" Angelica gasped.

He just flashed his sweet smile at her.

The dancefloor opened for other guests who wanted to share a dance so he asked, "Can I have this dance?" He extended his hand for hers to take.

Angelica was hesitant at first to take it, but she took the risk. She closed her eyes and held his hand putting her heart on the line once again as if she never learned from all the heartaches she'd experienced.

They stepped into the dance floor and faced each other. "You're getting pretty by the day," he commented.

"Tch. I don't get swayed by those kinds of compliments."

Adrian shrugged his shoulder, "I'm just stating facts."

"Since when did you become this bold when you hardly say your thoughts before?"

"I don't know. Maybe seeing you again made me regret how I acted in the past."

She didn't say anything and they just dance to the music enjoying each other's warmth. Angelica couldn't deny how much she missed him in just those six months that he was gone. Now, I'll take care of my heart first.

Stephen was also with Rosette sharing a precious moment with each other especially now that they were officially a couple. He introduced her to their colleagues in the party that she's his girlfriend. All were surprised since they knew Rosette as one of their patients at the hospital.

"I didn't expect you'd introduce me as your girlfriend already.

"Why? You didn't want to?" Stephen raised an eyebrow at her.

"Hmm..." She acted cute pretending to think, "No, I just thought it might put you at a disadvantage."

"Why?"

"Because you're dating a minor," she joked.

"Hey," he pinched her cheek with one hand while his other was still on her waist. "You're not a minor."

"Yeah, yeah, you're such a killjoy."

When the song ended the emcee stood on the stage again and told everyone, "To all the guests, we can have dinner now. Please wait to be called per table. And while we have our meal please enjoy a few dance numbers from our groom and bride. Please give them a round of applause."

Wearing a red dress and black high-heeled shoes, Jamaica stood in a pose at one edge of the dancefloor while Dereck, was wearing a white long-sleeved shirt in black pants and shoes.

The band played Por Una Cabeza by Itzhak Perlman and they began to groove to the rhythm.

Loud cheers and applause came from the audience, especially from Jamaica's friends since they didn't know she could dance. Mr. Sy, her parents, and Camila were getting excited about their performance.

Jamaica took steps slowly and then quickly made her way towards Dereck circling around him as she lightly placed her arms around his shoulder.

He never broke the gaze that he had since the start. He, too, moved by grabbing her by the waist and finally leading her to the dance.

Dereck couldn't see anyone else but her. His world was filled with just the two of them and that was more than enough. From the corner of his eye, he saw their daughter smiling and waving at them. He smiled thinking, Oh right I also have Camila. His smile turned into a smirk felt excited for what was about to happen later.

The song was about to come to an end so Dereck waited for the last movement then turned her around before tightening his hand around her waist. His right hand held her face, surprising her with a kiss.

All cheered inside the room as the unexpected scene unfold in their very eyes.

"I haven't said it to you, right?" Dereck asked.

"Huh?"

"That I love you," he smiled lovingly at her.

The smile that was only meant for her.

Instead of answering, Jamaica held his cheeks kissing him in return.

They were already in their hotel room taking a rest. Dressed in pajamas, both of them were lying on the bed and staring at the ceiling.

"I can't believe we're really in this new chapter of our life now," Dereck admitted.

He wasn't hearing any response from her so he checked if she was sleeping.

"Are you sleeping?" He poked her cheek. "Hey, you're not supposed to sleep on me." Dereck tickled her but she was dead asleep.

He sighed then got up to lay her down properly and placed a blanket on her. "Goodnight," Dereck kissed her on the forehead.

Relationships that were once broken were re-established by earned trust, understanding, and love for each other.

Theirs was one-of-a-kind and special because of the bond only the two of them share.

Her once dream was now a reality no one can take away from her.